Adult Life Skills for Children

for Children

– a fable

Eve Baker

Published by New Generation Publishing in 2022

First Edition

ISBN

	Paperback	978-1-80369-136-7
	Ebook	978-1-80369-137-4

www.newgeneration-publishing.com

 New Generation Publishing

A family of kittens living in Harrow learn about some of life's lessons with the help of their grandad, and some new friends.

-PROLOGUE-

The kittens were sitting around in the lounge. Shaky was sketching this family scene. He would have to put himself in the picture at some point. It would add to his collection of drawings. Grandad was on the sofa, reading the papers. His hair was, as usual, unruly, and he wore round glasses, making him look very intelligent. And he was too. PC had her headphones plugged into her ears and was working out some dance steps and counting numbers under her breath. The twins, Sly and Teddy, were tumbling around on the carpet. They were playing Connect Four when a tiny beam of light moving around on the floor and up the wall made them dart after it. Teabag, curled up next to Grandad, was reading a book. Mummy Cat was tidying up after lunch in the kitchen. It is Scooter who is weaving the light up and down the wall from a keyring torch, and the twins are obsessed with trying to capture it.

Grandad notices and sniggers. Teabag tuts and shakes her head before going back to her book. PC giggles. Sly turns to see what PC is laughing at and follows her gaze to Scooter. Teddy sees what Scooter is doing as well. They immediately pounce on him, and they all tumble around the room, knocking into PC. Suddenly, there are four kittens in a ball in the centre of the room. Shaky, who is sketching the scene, tries to distinguish between the two tiny black kittens that are Teddy and Sly. Sly has the cheekier face and Teddy has a slightly bigger spray of white fur under her chin. But they have to be together to tell the difference. Scooter looks the same as the twins, but black all over and bigger. PC has long black fur with a white tummy, and she has the long slim legs of a dancer. Teabag and Mummy Cat are both black and white and super-fluffy. All the kittens have orange eyes, except for Teabag and PC; their eyes are green.

Mummy Cat comes in and nestles between Grandad and Teabag on the sofa. She licks Teabag's head, who purrs. Reaching for the remote Mummy Cat turns on the TV and settles down to watch a quiz show. PC sits down on the floor, leaning against Grandad's knees. Strictly *will be on straight afterwards, and she never misses that. The twins settle back to playing Connect Four. Shaky has sketched the kittens tumbling in the middle of the room. He turns his attention to the sofa scene –Grandad, Teabag, Mummy Cat and PC; the fluffies, he calls them. He has the outline of them sketched out too. Where would he place himself? He is more tabby than black, for a start.*

Contents

CHAPTER ONE

The Bullies

On his way to school one morning, Scooter climbed onto a low bridge at the end of the park and watched the Yeading Brook flow swiftly along.

Scooter squeezed through the railings and jumped down along the bank. It had rained earlier that morning, so the tiny river's usual trickling was swollen. He decided not to go to school but to see where the small river went. He waved hello to a magpie sitting on a branch. She nodded and then flew off. Shortly, Scooter came to another small bridge. An arm of water came from the left and fed into the main steam. Scooter enjoyed scampering over the branches. The brook was never more than three metres across at its widest.

Further along, the water stopped flowing because a tree root had slipped down the bank and created a plug. Now the banks on both sides became steeper and muddier. Then the brook sucked through a tunnel that ran under a path overhead. Scooter jumped up. He could see that the water flowed through on the other side of the track. The trees and shrubs were thick. Their roots hung precariously exposed, and some trunks, snapped awkwardly through age or high winds, created bridges for him to leap onto to get further along.

After a while of leaping from branch to branch, the water stilled. Scooter was going to try and jump across. He felt that the water would only come up to his knees if he fell in, but he would not like that at all. Then he saw another fallen tree. Trotting across, he found himself on a muddy path.

Looking down, the brook flowed swiftly again. And then it stopped. Where did Yeading Brook go? And so Scooter changed his mind and went to school after all.

oOo

Near the school gates, he saw what appeared to be a clowder of four kittens surrounding Shaky, his younger brother, and to his horror, Shaky was handing over his money. Then the four slinks off down the road, Scooter caught up with Shaky, who was wiping away tears.

'Who were they?' Scooter demanded, but Shaky did not answer. Shaky blew his nose loudly and walked purposefully through the school gates.

oOo

Back at home Scooter confided in his younger twin brother and sister, Sly and Teddy. Sly wanted to get a knife and go to look for the muggers at once. Teddy did not think this was a good idea.

'Have you got a knife, Sly?' asked Scooter incredulously, holding out his paw for Sly to give it to him. After a moment, Sly reluctantly retrieved a long bread knife with a serrated edge from a box under the bottom bunk bed and gave it to him.

'Mummy Cat's been looking for this,' said Scooter. 'I'll put it back in the kitchen where it belongs.'

oOo

Next, Scooter went to talk to his older sister, Teabag.

'Look, Scooter, I am swamped with work right now. Our Shaky has low self-esteem, and he should sort himself out.' With that, she turned back to her studies, her fluffy tail taut with irritation.

Scooter sighed, feeling dismissed and at a loss as to what to do about Shaky, and for that matter, he did not know what Teabag meant by low self-esteem and so decided to find Grandad, to ask him about it. Grandad loved talking about cat behaviour and was always giving lectures about this and that. Grandad looked a bit like a mad professor, with long, long whiskers and round spectacles, and what's more, he was a scientist too. A psychologist to be precise. He loved to explain different types of behaviour and what caused things to happen. So, when Scooter asked him about self-esteem, Grandpa was only too happy to help.

'Self-esteem,' said Grandad, cheerfully. 'A sign of low self-esteem is when you don't think much of yourself. It is when you don't speak up and ask for what you want. You don't like to rock the boat. Other kittens' needs are more important than yours.'

Grandad continued, 'Imagine that the most influential cats in your life are those who take care of you, usually your parents, but you could have other cats caring for you. Therefore, what your parents or carers say to you has a powerful effect. What if your parents, for whatever reason, tell you: "Don't, stop it, be quiet" and so on, all the time? What could this do to your self-esteem?'

Scooter shrugged.

'It might make you feel unsure of yourself, a bit shy and scared to speak up for what you wanted. It could give you low self-esteem. What is self-esteem?'

'Um...' said Scooter, not sure what he could say.

'High self-esteem is when you feel good about yourself. Did you know that when you were born you had very high self-esteem? When we all were baby kittens, we never had a problem with demanding food, sleep, or being held. However, by the time we start school, something happens.'

'What happens?' gasped Scooter.

'How does low self-esteem happen?'

' Er...' began Scooter, confused.

Before Scooter could comment further, Grandad boomed on. 'It happens because we will have heard hundreds and hundreds of negative statements about ourselves from parents and other significant cats in our lives, such as grandparents and uncles and aunties, even older siblings. These are the "significant others." Peers and friends can also influence how we feel about ourselves as well. You may know what it is like to be bullied and teased by so-called friends.'

Scooter thought that he did his fair share of teasing as well, but he was not going to disclose that piece of information.

'These are some of the negative statements a significant other could say to you.'

With that, Grandad listed a whole stream of comments. Scooter flinched with each one.

'Shut up!'

'Be careful!'

'Idiot!'

'You are stupid!'

'Don't!'

'Stop it!'

'You are mad!'

'You can't!'

'Don't argue with me!'

'Kittens should be seen and not heard!'

'What will other cats think?'

'Eat up!'

'Go away!'

'Be quiet!'

'You've got to do this!'

'That's wrong!'

'Not now!'

'Get lost!'

'Who asked you?'

'Do what I tell you!'

'Stop showing off!'
'Respect your elders!'
'Don't get angry!'
'You are just like your uncle!'
'You are just like your aunt!'
'You are just like your brother!'
'You are just like your sister!'
'You are just like your father!'
'You are just like your mother!'
'Don't answer back!'
'Try this!'
'Silly cow!'
'Twit!'

'Do you hear any of these statements, Scooter?

Scooter thought it best not to interrupt Grandad's flow.

'Have you been called an idiot, stupid and asked what other cats will think? Being told to get lost and go away could make you feel unwanted or unloved or unappreciated.'

Scooter nodded.

Grandad continued. 'When parents compare you with others, not only does this give you an indication of what they think of you, but also what they expect of you in the long run. You're just like your father! You're just like your mother! You're just like your brother! You are just like your sister! You are just like your uncle! You are just like your aunt! Being compared to your aunt or uncle, etcetera, can make us think that we are "bad" because we learn that they do not like the cats they are referring to for some reason or other. Uncle is feral and your brother beats up mice, could be some of the comparisons. When we hear these words from cats who are supposed to love us and care for us, such as our parents, we believe them.'

The twins were always telling Scooter to shut up, and they tell each other to shut up too. Scooter thought that you could hear negative things every day, but you did not have to pay any attention to it all.

'I really must have high self-esteem,' he thought.

oOo

Scooter gathered his siblings and told them of his plan.

'We are going to follow Shaky to school. He must not see us. When the bullies surround him, we crowd around them quickly, so they don't escape. PC, you take a picture as evidence. Teddy and Sly, shout and scream at the top of your voices to unnerve them.'

Teddy and Sly screeched and hissed loudly.

'Fine,' continued Scooter, looking at the twins sharply to stop them. 'Teabag and I will give them a telling off, okay? Maybe get the money back. We will scare them so much, that they will think twice before they bully Shaky again or anyone else, for that matter.'

'So what do they look like?' asked PC.

'That's the thing,' said Scooter. 'I don't know.'

'So, how will we recognise them?' asked PC, confused.

'Well, there were four of them,' said Scooter thoughtfully, 'and then they were black and grey and ginger and tabby, and black and white and white and grey.'

'That's eight said Sly sceptically.

'Their faces had two colours,' said Scooter, trying to remember.

'Okay, what about eye colour?' asked PC.

'Er, said Scooter. 'I wasn't that close to them, but they seemed to have a blue eye and a green eye, and a green eye and yellow eye, and two blues eyes and, and, I am not sure, but we are still doing this, right?'

'They sound like they could be chimeras,' said Teabag.

'What do you mean?' asked Teddy.

'Well, I don't know too much, but it is something to do with having two types of DNA, and this is shown by their bi-colour coat, separated right down the middle. Google it!'

oOo

The next morning, Shaky left for school, and a few moments later, all the kittens left the house too. They kept an eye on Shaky, but nothing happened. No one came up to him. Every day for the next week or so, the kittens continued with their surveillance.

Sly was getting fed up with this. 'I'm not cut out to be a spy,' he said. 'I want to walk with my friends, and every day we have to walk to school as a family.'

'Nothing wrong with that,' said PC. 'You would want us to support you if something wasn't right, wouldn't you?'

'Yes but, it's nearly two weeks now, and maybe the muggers are not going to come back,' added Teddy.

'Maybe, maybe not,' said PC.
'Well we will be able to spot them at once,' said Sly sarcastically. 'There's four of them, right, and they are grey, black, white, tabby, ginger, with orange, blue and green eyes. Easy.'

oOo

At home, after dinner, Scooter called a meeting. They met in Grandad's den. Shaky was in the garden shed painting, and he had his headphones on with music blaring. He always went to bed early on school nights and would never dream of coming into the den after he'd finished painting.

'Well guys, we are trying to find the culprits who have made our brother's life miserable, and this has proved difficult. We can carry on for a bit more, or we can forget it,' said Scooter, looking at his siblings.

'Forget it said Sly.

'No,' said Teddy. 'We aren't losing anything by walking to school together. It's fun. I don't mind.'

'Yes but we are not walking with Shaky. Maybe that will upset him if he found out we were walking to school together without him.' said Sly.

'We never walked with him before. He would think it strange if we started walking with him now,' said Teabag. 'I do want to walk with my friends though, and I'd like to get to school earlier than you lot. We have been late a couple of times too. I am not waiting for any of you anymore if you can't be on time.'

Scooter listened to everyone and finally announced, 'I think we should continue for a bit more and that we should leave home earlier. That way, Teabag, you can meet up with your friends. You too, Teddy. And we can still watch out for Shaky.'

'I've got friends too,' retorted Sly. 'It's Shaky who has no friends.'

'He has us,' smiled PC.

'I hate bullies,' said Teddy. 'Why do they exist?'

'Bullies tend to have been bullied themselves,' offered Teabag. 'Maybe they have a horrible home life, and they are beaten and abused or something,' she added by way of an explanation.

'Or they are just nasty individuals,' chimed in PC.

'Yes, just nasty individuals, for no good reason,' thought Teddy sadly.

o0o

Then, one day, when Scooter seriously thought that they should go back to their old habits, they saw four skinny, short-coat kittens walk up to Shaky as bold as anything, wearing jeans and leather jackets.

'Are they the muggers?' whispered PC, suddenly scared.

The four kittens indeed had the strange colouring that Scooter described, albeit poorly, but you could see that the kittens were striking in the way they looked. The ringleader, the one who was now talking with Shaky, had one side of his face black, and the other side grey. One eye was blue and the other green.

'I think so,' said Scooter. 'There can't be many kittens looking like them. Start filming, PC. Come on, let's go.'

The siblings surrounded the four multi-coloured kittens. When Scooter nodded, the twins started meowing, but weakly, embarrassed, and stopped when all the kittens outside the school gates started looking at them.

'How dare you mug my brother! You should be ashamed of yourselves. We are going to take a photograph of you to the police and see what they have to say about it asserted Teabag.

'What?' asked the ringleader. 'Shaky, is this a joke?'

Before Shaky could answer, a teacher came rushing out of the school to see what the trouble was. 'What's going on here?'

Shaky and the strange-looking kittens walked off, leaving his brothers and sisters to explain the commotion.

o0o

Back at home, in the kitchen, Teabag was pacing the floor, her tail high and rigid. 'I have never been so embarrassed in all my life.' They had not seen Shaky all day. He had been in the art room at school. 'I won't be surprised if Shaky never speaks to us ever again.'

Suddenly, they heard the front door open, and slam shut. 'It's Shaky,' whispered Teddy. The kittens quickly pretended to be busy preparing snacks. The kitchen door opened. They all turned to see Shaky standing there with a rolled-up canvas under one arm, and a smear of black paint on his chin. He had a wide grin on his face. Shaky's siblings remained still. No one spoke.

'Okay, you guys. I know you meant well. Have a look at my painting.' Shaky unfurled the huge canvas to display the four kittens that they had seen earlier. All four of the kittens in the picture had two different colours of fur on their faces, split down the middle. They also had different coloured eyes.'

'Oh, you are so talented, Shaky. It's beautiful. Who are those kittens?' asked PC. 'They look so sweet.'

'You mean, the kittens you accused of mugging me? They are some models who agreed to pose for me for an art exam. I did my exam and I aced it. I passed, and I think they might take legal action.'

'That's not funny,' frowned Teabag.
Scooter was silent for a moment. 'But I saw them take your money and you were crying, Shaky.'

'It was not like that, Scooter. I asked them to sit for me, and they agreed, and when they came to say goodbye because I'd finished sketching them, they told me that their great-great-grandmother had died. I gave them some money to get some flowers. I knew her. I was crying because it was sad. They dropped by today to see the finished piece, and here it is.'

All Shaky's siblings looked at him blankly.

Grandad came into the kitchen and broke the silence.

'Oh, what a beautiful painting, Shaky. Chimeras. I can tell you all about chimeras.'

'It's okay, Grandad, Teabag told us,' said Scooter. 'We thought they were bullying Shaky.'

'It is chimeras that get bullied and stared at and called names like "two-face",' said Shaky. 'They were telling me about it when I was painting them.'

'Why are kittens so mean?' asked Teddy.

'Ignorant and stupid, I suppose,' said Shaky. 'I think I will call this painting *The Chimeras*.'

'Excellent,' said Grandad, helping himself to some water, and smiling broadly, surveyed the painting once more.

CHAPTER TWO

School's a Drag

It was bedtime. The twins were on top of their bunk beds, in pyjamas, still wide awake. They often had long conversations about different things before falling asleep.

'I'm not feeling this school malarkey,' sighed Sly. 'How long do we have to keep going there?'

'Every day,' said Teddy matter-of-factly.

'For how long?'

'Until we do our exams.'

'And then what?'

'We go to high school.'

'And then what?'

'We go to university.'

'And then what?'

'We get a job,' said Teddy, slightly irritated now.

'And then what?'

'We retire. Like Grandad.'

'And then what?'

'WE DO NOTHING — being retired means you don't have to work anymore. You can take up a hobby.'

'Well then, I am going to start a new hobby now. Then I don't have to go to school anymore, or university or get a job if that's how it all ends up anyway.'

Teddy giggled, despite herself.

'Seriously though. What are you good at, Sly?'

'You tell me because I don't know.'

'Shaky is a good artist. Teabag is academic. Scooter is okay at sports, and he is great with computers. PC loves dancing and acting. Sly, we have to find out what we are good at so that we can get a job that we love doing. I like reading, and I like shopping, I suppose.'

'I like eating,' offered Sly.

'I've got it, said Teddy, sitting up, all excited. 'Maybe I can be a fashion designer, and you can be a chef.'

'I could open a restaurant. You can make clothes. Scooter could make videos of our business to put online. We will be famous,' said Sly enthusiastically.

With that, the kittens jumped from their bunk beds. They held paws and started bouncing up and down and giggling.

Grandad popped his head around the door. 'Hey! You kitty cats should be asleep. You've got school in the morning.'

'Sly does not want to go to school anymore, Grandad, because it does not cater for his educational needs,' said Teddy, putting on a posh voice when she said "educational needs."

'I agree,' said Grandad.

The twins stopped jumping in surprise and clambered back into bed.

'I don't think you expected me to say that,' said Grandad.

Both Sly and Teddy shook their heads.

'Well, there are different types of intelligence. The subjects that people associate with being smart are maths, technology and the sciences.'

'Like Teabag? She's good at maths and science. She wants to be a doctor.'

Grandad nodded.

'However, you can be good at art,' said Grandad.

'Like Shaky?' said Teddy.

'Yes. Or dance and drama,' continued Grandad.

'Like PC?' said Sly.

'Yes,' said Grandad.

'You can have spatial intelligence,' said Grandad.

'What's that? asked Sly.

'If you are good at reading maps or putting together a flat-pack piece of furniture from a diagram, maybe'

'Scooter does that, ' said Teddy. 'He is good at computer games and sports and technical things.'

'Yes. If you excel in one area, you often find you are good in other areas too.'

'We don't know what we are good at, Grandad.'

'Yes, we do,' Sly reminded her.

'Oh yes, I am good at designing clothes and Sly is good at cooking. I am going to open my own business and so is Sly, a restaurant.'

'You know cooking involves maths, such as weighing and measuring, calculating cooking times and estimating temperatures. Cooking can be very technical. Baking is chemistry. Mixing ingredients and creating something new.'

'Wow,' said Sly, excited. 'I am a chemist.'

'Both those jobs, cooking and designing, are creative. You have to use your imagination to design clothes, Teddy, and to create lovely dishes, Sly.'

'And measure. Using a pattern probably involves spatial intelligence,' added Teddy, not to be outdone by Sly.

'I should think so,' said Grandad.

The kittens were thoughtful for a while.

'Here's a question for you,' posed Grandad. 'How would you increase your verbal intelligence?'

But all Grandad could hear was Sly softly snoring. Grandad tip-toed from the room, closing the door gently.

'Read more,' answered Teddy, under her breath, before falling soundly asleep.

o0o

At breakfast, Teddy said quite loudly to whoever was listening, 'Did you know that you could increase your intelligence? The principle is the same as increasing muscle strength. The more you work out, the larger your muscles become. If you do a sport often, you get fitter and fitter and hopefully better. If you read and study a lot, if you paint a lot, if you dance a lot, you can't help but improve. Brain cells never die; they just fade away from lack of use. Don't let your brain cells decay. Use it or lose it!'

'Well said,' said Grandad, beaming. 'I thought you were asleep last night before I finished talking to you.'

Sly wasn't sure how long into Grandad's talk he'd managed to stay awake for, but he was quite sure he'd heard most of it.

oOo

It was evening. Scooter knocked tentatively on the door of Grandad's den. Grandad was reading a psychological report about reaching your full potential.

'What's up, kitty cat?'

'I'm not feeling school either.'

'Like Sly?'

'Yes, but for different reasons,' said Scooter.

Grandad waited for him to continue.

'There are thirty kittens in my class, and I have to keep quiet all the time, or the teacher gets cross,' said Scooter, annoyed. 'I don't like working on my own; it sucks. We play sports in a team and support each other, but we have to be quiet and not help each other in the classroom, or our teacher accuses us of cheating.'

'But you are doing well, aren't you?'

'Yes but, if you do too well, they call you a geek.'

'Nothing wrong with being a geek,' said Grandad. 'Some of my best friends are geeks.'

'You'd get teased badly at my school ventured Scooter. 'It's not nice.'

'When schools are organised in the way they are, we start comparing ourself to others, and you can end up feeling bad,' said Grandad matter-of-factly.

'Is it that self-esteem thing again, Grandad?' asked Scooter.

'Precisely.'

Scooter lowered his head thoughtfully.

'Scooter, you have excellent interpersonal skills,' offered Grandad. 'You have lots of friends, and you want to do standup comedy and acting. That takes a lot of hard work and confidence, and you have to have a good memory for learning lines.'

'I know, but I am not sure if I'm any good at that.'

'It is a difficult one. Confidence is a difficult concept. You can be confident in one area and not so confident in other areas. You gain more confidence by practising and putting yourself out there. PC is always entering dance competitions.'

'She hates it when she doesn't win.'

'And she does more difficult dance routines every time, so she is always stretching herself.'

'I'll say,' said Scooter. 'It is part of her warm-up routine.'

Grandad smirked. 'Funny. What do you think are your talents and skills?'

'Dunno.'

'Well, a way to discovering what you think and know about yourself is to close your eyes.'

Scooter jumped onto an armchair, curled up and closed his eyes.

'In your mind's eye, picture yourself. Inside of your mind is your idea of who you are. That includes how you look, sound; your mannerisms and habits. How do you interact with others? Now, if the image of yourself is not the same as your ideal self, and the gap is vast, you will develop low self-esteem and lack confidence.'

'So, what do I do?'

'Stop comparing yourself to others. There will always be kittens cleverer or more handsome, or richer. Keep learning new skills. Be kind to yourself. Eat well and exercise regularly. Play. Drink lots of water. Don't smoke, drink alcohol or take drugs. Pretend. Start being. Plan carefully. Failure is not bad; it is learning what not to do. Keep yourself nicely groomed. You fake it until you make it.'

'Wow!' exclaimed Scooter. 'That's a lot to take in.'

'Learn to say no,' said Grandad sharply.

'What do you mean?'

'If someone asks you to do something you don't want to do, say no. Think about it by all means, but say no and mean it, if that's what you want. It takes a lot of confidence to maybe disappoint a friend or someone you respect, but you have to stay true to y o u r s e l f.'

'I will try that with the headteacher tomorrow, Grandad,' smiled Scooter.

'You know what I mean,' laughed Grandad. 'I don't want Miss Kitty phoning me saying that Scooter is misbehaving. Now, get yourself all the Bs: a beverage, bath and bed. Have you finished your homework?'

'Just a bit to do.'

'Get on with it.' Grandad was always kind and warm, but you had to do what you were told.

Scooter leapt from the armchair. 'Thanks, Gramps.' Scooter had a plan to do something that would be a challenge for him. He would have to think about it some more. Trying new things was scary, but he would fake it until he made it.

CHAPTER THREE

The Debate, the Dance, and the Art Exhibition

It was coming up to the Christmas break. Two weeks to go. During the last days of the school term, there were fewer lessons and more fun activities—the school play for a start. PC was in it; she was going to do a solo dance routine. She had been practising for weeks. Teddy had made her costume, and it was beautiful. Scooter was in the debating team, and he was the main speaker for the motion: *This house believes that you can determine your own future.* There had been regular tournaments around the neighbouring schools. Now the finals were between his school, Lionswood, and Linxton High.

Shaky's *The Chimeras* was part of the exhibition. Everyone said it was his best work yet. Some of the paintings had been sold and had a little red sticker on their frames. No one had bought Shaky's piece. The librarian displayed all the pictures in the school library, and guests would be encouraged to view them after the debate. Shaky would have to wait until the event to see who was coming and who would buy his artwork. It was exhilarating, nevertheless. If it did not sell, he would take it home and put it in Grandad's den, or give it to the four kittens who sat for the piece, or donate it to the school library. He could not decide.

oOo

The assembly hall filled with the kittens from Lionswood on one side and the kittens from Linxton trooped in behind their stern-looking teacher, a small, stocky cat with a stripy tail. Her glasses hung around her neck on a chain as she looked around haughtily. The two teams were already seated at the front on separate tables facing each other. Scooter was the team captain for Lionswood, and he would start the debate. Then the first kitten on the other team would speak, followed by the second kitten on Scooter's team, second on Linxton, the third on Lionswood, the third on Linxton. Finally, the fourth speakers would conclude and sum up for each group. There were probably one hundred kittens and teachers in the hall. The excited buzz was brought to a low mummer when Miss Kitty, the headteacher from Lionswood, came to the front.

'Welcome everybody,' she said, smiling. Everyone liked her. She could be stern, but mostly she was concerned with the welfare of each kitten and tried to help everyone to be better. Miss Kitty reminded everyone of an old saying: 'When they go low, you go high,' she would say, when referring to mean cats and bullies. Miss Kitty also taught psychology and encouraged the kittens to speak up in her class. She was interested in their ideas and thoughts. She'd started to teach debating skills so that no one spoke over each other or were rude. Scooter was the only one out of his friends who attended the debating sessions. They teased him a lot at first because they wanted him to play football instead, but now, they'd got used to it. Thursday lunchtime was debate time.

'First, I want to thank all the students and teachers of Lionswood for all the arrangements they made to host this event and welcome our visitors. I want to thank Linxton for taking up the challenge and being our guests this afternoon. I have seen you in action, and I know that you will be worthy opponents. But I have also seen my pupils in action, and they will give you a good run for your money.'

There were pockets of nervous laughter around the hall, mainly on the Lionswood side. The Linxtons were on their best behaviour because of the harsh looks their teachers gave them from time to time. They had got the "talk" before arriving. 'Anyone who lets Linxton down will be severely punished.'

Suddenly Scooter's mouth dried, and his legs started to shake a little. On the table in front of each debater was a saucer of water. Scooter lapped up the liquid thirstily. A kitten nearby on hosting duty refilled the saucer. 'Thanks,' mouthed Scooter silently.

'The debate will last for approximately thirty minutes. Each speech will be about three minutes, no more. You will hear a warning whistle when you have ten seconds to go.' Miss Kitty blew a whistle, which startled a few kittens. 'Then, we will take a vote. After the debate, we have snacks and drinks in the dining hall, prepared by our cookery class. The art exhibition is in the library, so do look at the splendid work we have there. It will give you all an opportunity to mingle. May the best team win! And without further ado, let us hear it for both teams.'

The auditorium erupted into loud cheering and clapping.

Miss Kitty raised her paw for silence and nodded at Scooter. This was the cue for him to begin. He rose onto his hind paws and clearing his throat began.

'Good afternoon my honourable toms and queens. Welcome to Lionswood School. We are delighted to host the finals of the debating heats. I want to congratulate Linxton for coming this far. The standard is quite high, and therefore Linxton, you should be proud to be runners up.' Scooter said this with a grin, but the challenge was there, nevertheless.

'This house believes that you can determine your own future. I say this because, from the moment we are born, we live out our lives according to a "script" like a play. Berne, who developed the theory of Life Scripts, said that most people live as if their whole life was pre-written. They are following a pattern that does not change in any way at all, from generation to generation. The village baker passes on the bakery to his oldest kitten. The farmer gives the farm to his kittens. The same farm he and his siblings inherited from his parents. Life is more flexible now, but can you see repetitions in your day-to-day life? Do you get up in the morning, go to school, come home, eat your dinner, watch TV, have an argument about homework and chores and what time to go to bed? Does this sound familiar to you?'

Scooter paused to observe some kittens nodding in the room. 'Will you be a doctor like your mother or work as a builder like your dad? Will you be an accountant like someone else in your family?' he continued. 'If you can recognise a pattern, you are living out a Life Script,' said Scooter emphatically, banging down on the table. 'Scripts can be tragic, epic, adventurous, a soap opera, even a comedy. You can recognise a Life Script because of the repetition. My argument is, if you recognise and understand your Life Script, you can rewrite it. You can change it. It won't always be easy, but it can be done, if you don't like how it is going, or how it will end up. There is evidence to support this. Cats can change their so-called destiny.' Scooter made quote signs with his paws when he said the word "destiny." 'I will give you an example. A local cat found a clowder of kittens abandoned in a box. All those kittens could have become strays, living on the streets. That was their destiny, you might say. Indeed, most of those kittens did become feral. A life of crime, fighting, hunger. But one of them didn't. That one kitten grew up to do something no one in her family had ever done, and now she is the headteacher of Lionswood High School for Cats. May I introduce you to Miss Kitty, our headteacher?' Scooter threw his front paws open and turned towards Miss Kitty.

Miss Kitty bowed her head, embarrassed, and then looked up, smiling, proud of her achievements.

The whole auditorium erupted into applause that went on for some minutes.

'Some kittens live out a "good" Life Script, and some live out a "bad" Life Script.' Scooter drew invisible quote signs in the air again. 'My question is, which do you want? Because this house believes that you can determine your own future.'

With that, Scooter sat down to more rapturous applause. He sipped some water from the saucer in front of him. The first speaker on the Linxton team got up to speak, but she did not have a good argument.

At the end of the debate, Lionswood was triumphant winners. Even most of Linxton voted for Lionswood. Scooter jumped on the table, holding the winner's cup above his head, and quickly jumped down again when he saw Miss Kitty shake her head. 'There are refreshments in the dining hall. Let's eat, folks,' shouted Scooter above the chatter. 'And the art exhibition is in the library.'

'Congratulations, Scooter,' beamed Miss Kitty. 'If I knew you were going to use me as an example, I would have discouraged you, but it seems to have done the trick. We won. Good job.'

'Thanks, Miss Kitty. I'm sorry if I embarrassed you, but your story was perfect for making my point.'

'Indeed. I will have to scrutinise your debate speeches more closely in the future. Run along.'

oOo

A kitten from Linxton came up to Scooter and said, 'This is for our school magazine. To what do you owe Lionswood's success in the debating tournament?'

Scooter thought for a moment and replied, 'You have to have a good point first of all. Then you explain what you mean, and then you give some excellent examples, and statistics if you have them – anything relevant, and accurate. And finally, you have to link back to your original point. Your speakers could have come up with more examples. They never even looked at the audience either, and they spoke too quickly and not loudly enough for the kittens at the back to hear. Even the worst arguments can be won with the right body language and engagement with the audience. But Linxton did well getting this far.'

'I suppose,' said the Linxton kitten, downhearted.

'It works with essays too. If you have schoolwork, I mean. You know, debating techniques orders thinking and gets you better marks. It's not just for debaters,' offered Scooter. He did not want the Linxton kitten to feel bad.

'Thanks, Scooter,' said the Linxton kitten.

'No problem,' said Scooter, glad to be of help. 'Will I see you at next year's tournament?'

The Linxton kitten nodded half-heartedly, before sauntering off into the crowd.

oOo

Visitors had an opportunity to view the art exhibition almost all of December. The school had sold virtually all the paintings, mostly to parents who wanted to support their own kittens. The school invited the local mayor as well as all the parents and the artists to the opening of the exhibition. Grandad and Mummy Cat turned up with Shaky reluctantly in tow. Shaky hated all this. Grandad thought that he would bid for Shaky's painting if no one came forward. He saw that there was no red sticker on the frame. The mayor officially opened the event and led the viewing in his official crimson cloak and gold chains. He stopped at each painting and asked the artist questions such as, 'How long did it take you to paint?' and 'What was the motivation for your work?'

There was red and white wine for the adult guests, and some of the older school kittens came around with canapés. Some kittens had decorated the school library with flowers and Christmas lighting that made it look quite impressive—the queens dressed in long evening gowns and the toms in tuxedos. Everyone looked elegant. Mummy Cat and Grandad beamed with pride when the mayor came to talk to Shaky.

'It took me the whole term to paint this because there were four kittens. Kieran, Isaac, Isaiah, and Nathan. I wanted to bring out their characteristics and features. They are quite beautiful, with lovely fur and amazing eyes,' blurted out Shaky, before the mayor even spoke to him.

'You certainly did that, young cat. And what was your motivation?'

Shaky believed he'd answered that question, but thought about it some more and said, 'Those four kittens have a tough life. Some cats feel that they are gang members because of how they dress. Jackets, jeans, trainers, but they are just friends hanging out. Cats should not judge and make assumptions. They are always getting stopped and searched by police cats.'

Miss Kitty rang a bell, and everyone stopped talking and turned to look at her. 'I hope that you all have had a drink and something to eat. We have kittens here at Lionswood who have an excellent range of talent. We won the debate tournament. Lovely. Next week we have our performance. I hope you all can attend. Tickets are still on sale. And tonight you can see what talented artists we have here too. We have sold all the paintings, bar one. It is the painting entitled *The Chimeras* by Shaky. Or rather, should I say, there has been a bidding war over this painting.' There was a gasp from the attendees and a buzz of excitement. 'We have invited the three bidders to place their proposal in an envelope, and the top bidder will take the painting home. Can I invite the mayor to open the envelopes?'

'It would be my pleasure. I can't say I have done anything like this before.' Taking an envelope from a tray Miss Kitty held out, the mayor proceeded to open it.

'This is from the local museum. They bid five hundred pounds. That is very generous. Very generous indeed.'

The second envelope was from Lionswood itself.

'For the school library,' offered the librarian. It was for ten pounds.

'It would be nice to keep this wonderful painting here,' said the mayor. 'But alas, not enough.'

When the mayor opened the third and final envelope, he had to sit down. He took out a handkerchief and wiped his brow. 'I am not sure if this is correct,' he said, showing the contents to Miss Kitty. She sat down too.

There was silence in the library. All waited for the mayor to speak. He cleared his throat, stood up again, and then told everyone that they had a bid for five thousand pounds.

Shaky burst into tears.

oOo

The last week of the term came. The first night of the school play was on Wednesday, followed by a performance on Thursday and Friday; a matinee on Saturday afternoon and the last performance on Saturday evening. The show was about two rival gangs that hated each other; the Cool Cats and the Purple Panthers. The poster for the Cool Cats had a yellow emoji face with sunglasses and four cat emojis.

The Purple Panthers had to have the words written under the picture of a purple panther because it was not apparent that it was a panther. It could have been a leopard, or a tiger or a jaguar painted purple.

PC was first on stage. The spotlight was on her.

Suddenly, James Brown's voice screamed.

> *Whoah! (Bop!) I feel good,*
> *I knew that I would now.*
> *I feel good,*
> *I knew that I would now.*
> *So good, so good, I got you.*
>
> *I feel nice, like sugar and spice,*
> *I feel nice, like sugar and spice.*
> *So nice, (bop, bop),*
> *So nice (bop, bop),*
> *I got you.*

PC, dressed in a blood-red velvet catsuit, moved rhythmically to the beat, c-walking, shuffling and sliding, reminiscent of the Godfather of Soul in his heyday. She scrunched down, seemingly exhausted as the music died down. Another dancer came out of the stage wings and put a cape around PC's shoulders and tried to lead her away. The audience was worried. PC had danced so energetically, no wonder she was tired. PC started to walk away with the support of the other dancer, when suddenly, halfway across the stage, she tossed the cape away. The volume of the song crescendoed.

So good, so good, I got you.

PC started dancing just as vigorously as before.

> *So good, so good,*
> *I got you.*
> *So good, so good,*
> *I got you.*
> *Hey!*

PC ended with the splits in true James Brown style.

The audience was on their feet, clapping and cheering—what a start to the show.

CHAPTER FOUR

The Kittens Meet a New Friend

'Should we go out to explore at night or in the daytime?' asked Teddy.

'Well we are nocturnal by nature, and we can see very well in the dark. Let's go tonight said Scooter.

'I can't go. I have work to do. In any case, I'm crepuscular. I do my best work at dawn and dusk.' Flicking her tail, Teabag walked off, back to her room.

'I'm not up to it either because I'm diurnal said Sly, mocking Teabag's tone and flicking his tail as he curled up on an armchair, yawning and stretching.

'I have to practise a new dance,' said PC. 'You go. Have fun.'

'So, it's just us two Teddy,' said Scooter.

They did not even bother asking Shaky.

It was on that trip that Teddy and Scooter met Milo. He was mostly white and short-haired with a sweet perky face. He had a black nose and black eyes that resembled large coat buttons, in a triangular face. His ears were triangles too, and his head was the shape of an apple. Teddy found him enchanting.

Milo often went to the park. He walked there every day. More importantly, he knew where the Yeading Brook went, and he was delighted to show the kittens the way.

'And, over there is a nature reserve' he said excitedly.

'Really?' said Scooter.

'You can only get to it from that corner of the park' said Milo, starting to lead the way.

The kittens and Milo hiked down a path because the grass was soggy. Milo did not like getting his feet wet. Then they turned right along another track. Scooter and Teddy could see the back of their school, and three houses along was their house. The bedroom windows were open, and they could see glimpses of their garden through the slats of the fence.

'We live there' said Scooter, pointing out their house.

'Lucky you, living so close to your school. I have to walk quite a bit, but it's a mixed school. Cats, dogs, birds and squirrels go there.'

'Cool,' said Teddy. 'I would like that. Ours is just kittens.'

They walked a little further and then found there were two paths.

'If we take the left paw path, we can explore the brook, and if we keep to the right, we will get to the nature reserve,' advised Milo.

This night-time excursion was more exciting than Scooter and Teddy had dreamed.

'There are ducks and frogs in the reserve,' said Milo enthusiastically. 'What's it to be? Brook or nature reserve?'

'Nature reserve,' said Teddy and Scooter together.

Milo trotted in front quickly, but the kittens had no trouble keeping up with him.

'I love nature,' said Milo sniffing a tree and then another, and another.

'I do too,' Teddy decided.

Scooter looked at her. He was not aware of her love of nature before this.

After a while exploring, they did not see any frogs or ducks. It was getting late, so they had to go home.

'The ducks only come out in the day, and the frogs are probably hibernating,' said Milo knowledgeably.

'Would you like to come to tea?' blurted out Teddy, finding Milo super smart.

'Um… Okay,' said Milo, surprised, but pleased.

Teddy made the arrangements, and Milo noted the address.

They said their goodbyes and on parting, Milo shouted, 'Four o'clock!'

'What was that?' asked Scooter.

'I invited him round for tea,' said Teddy.

'Cool said Scooter, pleased they had made a new friend.

oOo

Everyone was in the kitchen when Milo arrived. Teddy opened the door and led him into the kitchen. Sly had set the table with sausages, and fish and beef biscuits. Sly was putting some barbecued chicken on the table and turning to greet Milo immediately started snarling, hissing and with an arched back, extended his claws.

'Calm down, Sly,' said Teddy. 'This is Milo.'

'He's a dog,' snarled Sly.

'Well done for observation,' said Teabag sarcastically.

'Now, now, Sly. What have I taught you about tolerance?' said Grandad, sighing heavily.

'He's a dog,' hissed Sly.

Milo's smile dropped. A low growl escaped from his throat, but he immediately corrected himself, pretending to cough, and said, 'Hello Sly. I've heard all about you. They say you are an excellent chef. The food certainly smells delicious. I am so pleased to meet you.'

Milo extended a paw in greeting.

Sly, looking at him for a moment, turned and stormed off, tail rigid in the air.

'Oh dear, I do apologize for my grandson's behaviour,' said Grandad. 'It is nice to meet you, Milo. Tell us something about yourself. Sit, sit.'

Milo was very hungry. He licked his lips and was trying hard not to drool.

'It's okay,' said Grandad, reading his mind. 'It reminds me of a friend of mine, Pavlov. He had dogs that would salivate every dinner time. The sound of a bell also accompanied mealtimes. Later on, the dogs would salivate just to the sound of the bell.'

'Yes', said Milo. 'That was a significant psychological study. We learned the history of the dogs who worked with Pavlov at school. The dogs, Rosa, Mirth, Bierka, Ikar, to name but a few, spent a lifetime advancing the study of conditioning and behaviour. It is just as easy to learn good habits as it does bad ones.'

Grandad beamed. 'What a clever champ you are, Milo. Tuck in.'

'Tell us about yourself Milo,' said PC. 'Where do you come from?'

'Well, I was born here, of course. My parents are Mexican.'

'*¿Hablas español?*' asked Teabag. She was learning Spanish and loved practising at every opportunity.

'*Sí, un poco. Pero ahi hablamos Tarahumara.*' That's what's mostly spoken in the Chihuahua area of Mexico. That's where my ancestors come from, and we are the smallest breed of dog in the world,' said Milo proudly.

'Interesting,' said PC. 'And you come from a little place called Chihuahua?'

'Chihuahua is bigger than the UK,' said Milo, slightly annoyed.

It was then that they noticed Scooter was not at the table. He had gone to find Sly.

Sly was in the garden, still furious.

'What's your problem? When did you get so bigoted? Weren't we brought up to be tolerant of others and be kind to mice and rats?'

'I like playing with mice,' sulked Sly.

'They don't like it.'

'They don't mind.'

'Yes, they do,' said Scooter emphatically. 'Playing with them is just exploitation for the gratification of cats. That's why we don't have toy mice anymore.'

'Grandad had one when he was a kitten. He told me,' said Sly defiantly.

'The world was different then. We know better now. Come on, Sly. Would you like it if someone hated you just because you were a cat? For no other reason? And then made up stories to justify hurting you?'

'No,' said Sly, shocked.

'Well, then?'

'I'm sorry. It was just a surprise. I didn't expect Milo to be a dog.'

'You did not come with us on the trip last night. Milo is a good friend. Come on; you're missing a lovely feast,' cajoled Scooter.

'I know. I cooked it. '

Moments later, both Sly and Scooter slid back into their seats around the dining table.

Sly noticed Milo's plate was empty.

Milo was trying to be polite, but he could have demolished the entire chicken.

'Have some more, Milo,' said Sly, noticing Milo eyeing the chicken and by way of an apology as well.

'Yes, please, it's delicious. I think you should open a restaurant.'

'Funny you should say that' said Sly with a grin.

'Milo was telling us about the green parakeets that go to his school,' said Grandad.

'Yep,' said Milo, swallowing a morsel of the meal, continued with his story. 'Buz and Lu's great-great-great-great times twenty or more maybe, grandparents came to England from Asia to star in the film *African Queen* with Humphrey Bogart, a famous Hollywood actor. The parakeets met, fell in love and flew away when the filming was over. JimJam's ancestors used to sing harmonies with Jimi Hendrix, a rock guitarist. When they heard about the parakeet actors, the parakeet singers left the band, and they all lived together in the trees of West London. Now there are hundreds of parakeets all over the place. All those parakeets you see are the descendants of Buz and Lu and JimJam's forebears.'

oOo

At bedtime, Grandad came in to say goodnight to the twins. 'You know, when I was growing up, we lived in a house with Max. He was as big as an Alsatian. My mum, your great-grandma, thought of him as her brother, they were so close. They did have arguments sometimes, but Max would let me and my siblings jump all over him, and we would all sleep in the same basket. I remember my mum boxing Max's nose one morning because he was sniffing around her breakfast. Max could have eaten my mum in one gulp, and all of us kittens in another. But he knew he was out of order and backed off. We all loved him. Knowing Max, and Milo and the green parakeets allow us to be receptive to new experiences and ideas. I am glad you came back into the kitchen, Sly.'

'Me too, Grandad. I like Milo. And anyone who loves my cooking is a good friend.'

CHAPTER FIVE

The Fire Alarm

'You're not my mum,' retorted Sly.

'BE QUIET! You moan all the time,' reprimanded Teabag.

'I don't,' snapped Sly.

'Well, eat your breakfast and hurry up,' replied Teabag, stomping her paws.

Grandad chuckled. 'I can see the ego states at work here.'

'What, Grandad?' asked Scooter.

'Watch. Listen to how Teabag is talking to Sly. And then see what Teddy does.' Grandad started to whisper as if he was commenting on wildlife in the forest and did not want to disturb them.

Scooter was not sure what Grandad was getting at. Arguing at breakfast was not unusual. Someone would eat all the cereal or not put the milk back in the fridge, or something.

Just then, Teddy went up to hug Sly. 'There, there, Sly, you don't have to eat it if you don't want to.'

'You will be hungry later on,' hissed Teabag.

'I don't care,' sulked Sly, ignoring Teddy.

'Why don't you make a sandwich of it and take it for your lunch?' suggested Teddy.

'Oh, that's a good idea. I will do that.' Sly stuck his tongue out at Teabag.

'Teabag is in a Parent ego state, critical Parent ego state, I might add. Teddy comes along, also in the Parent ego state but the nurturing Parent ego state. Sly is in the Child ego state; quite rebellious. But then both he and Teddy solved the problem of what to do with breakfast; have it for lunch. This transaction is the Adult ego state. The Adult ego state is being sensible and about problem solving. We communicate all the time from one of three ego states and can switch at any time. You do not have to be a parent to be in the Parent ego state, nor do you have to be an adult to communicate from the Adult ego state, and anyone can behave childishly.'

'But then Sly did a very childish thing, didn't he, by sticking his tongue out?' asked Scooter.

'There is no way Sly is going to behave like an adult for too long,' chuckled Grandad. 'Nor should he. Or anybody. It is all about appropriateness. If your behaviour is inappropriate, it will cause a crossed transaction and be annoying. It could make an argument last longer. If Teabag saw him stick his tongue out, it might have led to another row.

oOo

It was evening, and Scooter went to see his grandad. When I go to get my hair cut, I want my barber to look after me and offer me a nice saucer of cream.'

'Cream? Not milk, Grandad?'

'My barber is very expensive. I tip very well, so I expect cream.'

'What ego state are you in when you demand cream, Grandad?'

'Probably the Little Professor.'

'But you are a professor.'

'Sure, but everyone can be cunning and clever, and manipulative, in a good way, even a tiny kitten. That is the Little Professor at work in the Child ego state. Of course, it is best to be in the Adult ego state mostly, but being playful is fine. To be polite and respectful is good. Parents like little kittens to say please and thank you. However, if there were a fire, I wouldn't have a problem with you making sure that we got out of here, unharmed.'

'EVERYONE GET UP AND GET OUT INTO THE GARDEN, IMMEDIATELY.

DON'T BOTHER TAKING ANYTHING WITH YOU,' shouted Scooter.

oOo

Grandad was giving more examples for some time when they heard some meowing from outside. Scooter ran to the window and leaned out.

'Can we come in now?' wailed Teddy.

'We've been out here for ages, and it's cold.'

'What are you doing out there?'

'You told us to,' said Mummy Cat, in a huff, still in her dressing gown, her head in a turban and a face pack smothered over her face, set hard, so she could hardly move her mouth.

'Yes, yes, come in. Good job, everyone. I was testing the fire drill. What's that you've got there, Sly?'

'My phone.'

'Teddy?'

'My designs.'

'Teabag?'

'My books.'

'PC? What have you got with you?'

'Nothing. I went to fetch Mum.'

'Well, you have all failed, except PC of course.'

'I told you not to take anything with you. If it was a real fire, it could've been dangerous.'

'Can we come in now?' Sly stamped his paws on the ground.

'Yes', said Scooter, closing the window quickly.

'You got away with that this time,' said Grandad sniggering like a kitten. 'Keep your voice down next time.'

'Don't worry, Grandad. I think I learned my lesson but it was fun being in my Adult ego state.'

'Yes, it suits you. The Adult ego state is closely linked to assertiveness as well, but that's another story.'

oOo

'Well now, school is over. It will be Christmas in a few days. Has everyone got their presents?' asked Mummy Cat.

'We agreed not to spend too much money,' said PC.

'I don't have any money,' said Sly. 'I'm cooking and making loads of cakes for everyone.'

'That's nice,' said Teddy. 'I don't like Christmas cake though or pudding. I like carrot cake and lemon drizzle.'

'I'm going to make what everyone likes, one big cake each.'

'I've made everyone an outfit, but you can't see what it is until Christmas morning,' said

Teddy, excitedly. 'You know what you are getting, because I had to measure you up, but it will still be a surprise.'

'Do you think we should invite Milo for lunch?' suggested Sly. 'It will be nice to have him here.'

'That's a splendid idea', said Grandad, pleased that Sly had got over his prejudice and was so welcoming and friendly towards Milo now.

oOo

Christmas Day arrived bringing with it a grumpy sky that angrily spattered rain upon all the houses and anyone silly enough to be outside in it. Scooter's family were indoors, snug and warm. The aroma emanating from the kitchen was intoxicating. Milo had arrived the night before and slept in Scooter's bed, while Scooter bedded down in a big basket. Scooter didn't mind.

'That way he can have breakfast with us too,' reasoned Scooter.

'And we can play games,' added Sly.

'What has Sly the Tolerant decreed this time?' said Teabag, laughing. 'Is Milo your BFF?'

'Grandad says that sarcasm is indirect aggression,' offered Sly.

Breakfast was simply oatmeal and milk. Milo came into the kitchen, wiping his mouth with a tissue. He was salivating again. How embarrassing.

'Thank you for having me,' he said to Mummy Cat.

'Not at all, you are most welcome. Sit down and eat your breakfast, then we can open presents.'

oOo

Teabag got books. Everyone got a laptop from Grandad and Mummy Cat. Even Milo got a laptop computer. He burst into tears when he opened the box.

'Sly suggested it,' said Teddy, 'for being so horrid to you.'

'Stop rubbing it in,' said Sly, embarrassed. 'I, oh, never mind. Sorry.'

Milo hugged Sly, and that was the end of it.

'Can I keep it here?' asked Milo. 'For safety.'

The kittens thought that strange, but agreed.

Teddy handed out her gifts to everyone. There was an assortment of knitted jumpers, scarves and an evening dress for Mummy Cat made from altering two older dresses that Mummy Cat no longer wore.

'This is so beautiful, Teddy. I love it. You have made it into something unique and special,' beamed Mummy Cat, holding the dress up.

Teabag, Shaky, PC and Scooter had not bought anything for any of the kittens, because they'd agreed to contribute to the laptops so that Milo could get one. All the kittens knew this and were happy about the arrangement. Teddy and Sly were exempt because Sly cooked and Teddy made outfits. Teabag got the books she wanted because she was studying. It would be university this year if she got the right grades.

'I got something for you, Milo,' said Teddy, handing him a small box wrapped in tissue and ribbons.

Milo opened the box carefully and was surprised to see inside four teeny-tiny little boots.

'Put them on, put them on,' squealed Teddy, jumping up and down. 'Aren't they the cutest thing?'

Milo wasn't sure. He'd never worn anything on his paws before. He put them on hesitantly, with the help of the kittens doing up each boot.

'You'll have to come round every morning to help me put them on,' laughed Milo.

'Well, you don't like getting your feet wet.'

'That's true,' said Milo.

'So when I saw the pattern, I had to make them for you, and I embroidered a letter of your name on each shoe. L O M I. You have to put them on the right way, so they spell M I L O, Milo, but it doesn't matter.' Milo could not see how the letters would spell out his name, no matter which way he put the boots on.

'I will have to get used to them though. Thanks,' said Milo, still unsure.

Then there was a slinky mini dress with fringing around the bottom.

PC squealed with glee. 'Just what I wanted for my salsa routine. How did you know?'

'I am not deaf, PC. I can hear you playing Cuban music in the living room where you go to work out your routines. I like the music. It's cheerful,' Teddy added, just in case PC thought her music disturbed her.

'Salsa is a wonderful dance, but I may have to give up because I can't find a partner and you do need a partner for salsa, and rumba and the cha cha cha.' PC swayed to some imaginary music in her head.

'I can salsa,' said Milo.

Everyone's heads snapped around quickly to look at Milo, mouths agape with surprise.

PC quickly left the room and came back with some music. She pressed play, and the room was filled with Los Van Van's song, *Timpop Con Birdland*. Milo, knowing all the words, took PC's paw, and they danced, and he sang along. His voice was surprisingly good. Milo spun PC around, lifted her in the air and then he did some intricate steps while shaking his shoulders. Milo let PC go, and they both solo danced, but still synchronised before dancing in partnership again.

'I should have put on my new dress. You are the best salsa dancer, ever, Milo.'

Everyone agreed, clapping.

o0o

'It's time for Christmas dinner,' shouted Sly from the kitchen. 'Let's eat.'

CHAPTER SIX

The Accident

'We're supposed to be meeting Milo here. He's late,' said Scooter, irritated. 'He would have come in at the south gate because I think he lives that way. Let's go there and wait for him.'

Teddy and Scooter waited for some time and were walking back home the other way around the park when they heard a commotion.

'What are they doing?' Teddy pointed to a parliament of magpies, screeching and squawking and running around busily. Just then, they spied a tiny leg, and a little boot in the middle of the flock.

'That's Milo,' shouted Scooter in alarm.

When the kittens approached a few of the birds flew up into the air, but then they came back down.

One of the magpies said defensively, 'We didn't hurt him, we found him like this. He'd stopped breathing.'

Teddy gasped. 'Is he dead?'

'Dead? No. He's breathing now. We pecked him awake. But we think he broke a leg, maybe. He has to get to the hospital. I'm

Maggie Magpie, by the way. I saw you the other day, down by the brook.'

'No hospital rasped Milo, suddenly more alert and trying to sit up. 'I don't want to go to the hospital. My leg's not broken. I just sprained it, I think.'

'Well someone needs to look at it to make sure,' said Maggie Magpie assertively.

'I know,' said Teddy. 'Let Teabag look at it. Your ear; it's bleeding, Milo.'

'Can you stand up?' asked Scooter.
'I think so.' Milo tried. 'Ouch!' He sat back down.

'We can fly you to Scooter's house. It's quicker,' offered Maggie Magpie.
Before Scooter or Teddy could comment, Maggie Magpie whistled and a few more birds appeared. Some of the birds grabbed hold of Milo's collar, others the back of his jacket, the trouser loops where a belt should go with their beaks and lifted Milo into the air. What a sight. If Milo weren't so ill, he would have enjoyed the ride, once he'd got over his initial trepidation. If there were ever a next time, he would keep his eyes open. Milo was lifted high above the trees, the road and houses and was set down by the birds at the kittens' front door. Teddy picked up Milo's boot, the one that had fallen off and both he and Scooter raced

around on the ground and got home in time to see the birds in the sky heading back to the park. Scooter and Teddy waved and shouted thanks to the magpies.

'You saved our friend,' shouted Scooter at them as they disappeared from view.

Teabag heard the commotion outside, and when she opened the door, Milo fell into her arms.

'Oh, you poor thing. Come into the living room. Let's have a look at you. I can see you're hurt. What happened?'

Milo gave a weak smile and said, 'I was practising walking in my new boots and I slipped on some wet grass along the bank of the brook. I banged my head on a rock or tree trunk and passed out, I suppose. The magpies woke me up and then Scooter and Teddy came along.'

'Milo is your first patient, Teabag,' smiled Teddy. 'We can be assistants.'

'Okay then,' nodded Teabag. 'Hot water, Scooter, in a bowl. Teddy, towels, bandages and disinfectant. And two cups of sweet, milky tea.'

'Two cups?'

'One for me and one for Milo. Quick, quick.'

Milo propped himself up on pillars on the sofa, his ear bandaged and a packet of frozen peas taped to his bad leg. Teabag had placed three boots neatly in a corner.

'Oh dear, I think I'm missing a boot.'

'Don't worry, I've got it here,' said Teddy.

'Do you think those boots are a good idea, seeing that Milo nearly broke his neck?' asked Scooter sharply.

'I can put something on the bottom to stop them being slippery,' offered Teddy.

'Perhaps,' said Milo. 'Or I should get used to getting my feet wet. I don't want to hurt your feelings, Teddy.'

'Not at all,' said Teddy, but you could see she was upset. 'I don't want you to break your neck either,' she said, tearfully, running from the room.

oOo

Milo had a good night's sleep on the sofa.

Teabag checked on his leg the next day and could see that the swelling was hardly there. She removed the bandage around Milo's ear.

'I am just going to clean the wound. I don't want it to get all infected, and then you will be fine.'

'You have been super kind, Teabag. Thank you. Er, your name is a bit unusual. Why do they call you Teabag?'

'Oh, it's no mystery. When I was born, I was no bigger than a packet of tea. That's all. And then a tea bag fell on the floor, and I played with it until all the tea came out and made a mess. I don't know what the truth is. And the other story is that I use to hide teabags behind the washing machine. Don't worry, I don't do any of that anymore,' laughed Teabag, noticing the look Milo gave her.

'I need to thank the magpies for saving me.'

'You can do that when you are all better said Teabag. 'It's chicken soup for lunch.'

Milo felt so happy and so hungry all at the same time.

oOo

The kittens slurped their soup and gnawed the chicken bones. Sly was delighted that they were enjoying it so much. Even Mummy Cat and Grandad were smacking their lips and helping themselves to more.

After the meal, PC, Shaky, and Teabag went off, leaving Scooter, Sly, Teddy, Mummy Cat, Grandad, and Milo sitting around the dining table in silence.

'I am hoping for another dog in the White House,' said Milo, by way of conversation.

'There was never a dog in the White House,' said Scooter incredulously.

'Yes, there was. Lots, over the years. Bo, Bernie, Charlie, Buddy, Millie, Champ,' said Milo, listing all those he could remember.

'We've had cats in Downing Street. Great leaders of our country,' offered Grandad. 'Munich Mouser was the greatest during the war years and adviser to Winston Churchill himself. Larry is a disaster. I remember him having a big row with Palmerston, the Foreign & Commonwealth Office cat. Larry fabricated some nonsense to get us out of Europe. I will be glad to see the back of him.'

'Let's not talk politics,' said Mummy Cat, fearing the brewing of an argument. 'We don't know what role Larry played.'

'Peter worked with Stanley Baldwin, and it was his idea to start the National Health Service. Other cats developed the health services further. They were great politicians,' continued Grandad, ignoring Mummy Cat.

'There is a dog in Number 10 now,' offered Scooter.

'Sure but he has not said much. I will be glad to see the back of him too,' said Grandad. 'He's too young. In any case Larry is still in office.

That new dog, dopey Dilyn, is a political strategy to oust Larry.'

'Will you stop?' repeated Mummy Cat.

'They say that there have been no mice in the White House or Number 10. They are the unsung heroes. They work in the back rooms turning nonsense policies into actions we can work with,' said Grandad, moving the conversation away from cats and dogs.

'Seems like cats have been at the forefront of science and politics,' said Sly, helping himself to a slice of bread to mop up the last of his soup. Mummy Cat glared at him.

'Not just cats and dogs. Do you know that a cow discovered a vaccine for cowpox which was adapted to cure smallpox?' said Grandad, attempting to move the discussion to other unsung heroes.

'Laika was the first dog to orbit the earth in space, but Albert, a monkey, went on a sub-space trip back in 1948,' stated Milo matter-of-factly, not looking at Mummy Cat. 'We learnt that at school.'

'I give up,' said Mummy Cat, sighing, and shaking her head.

CHAPTER SEVEN

No Caller ID

'Hello.'

A disembodied voice continued, 'I am calling on behalf of Felix. The international art dealer. He would like to talk to you. I am putting you through now.'

Shaky knew who he was. It was he who had bought his painting at the school's Christmas exhibition. Felix had paid five thousand pounds for *The Chimeras.*

oOo

Shaky came bounding into the living room where PC was dancing the bachata with Milo to a song by Aventura, a Dominican band.

'Guess what?' said Shaky excitedly.

The two stopped dancing. PC and Milo could see his excitement, and, more importantly, they had never seen Shaky so animated. It was a surprise. Shaky was shaking.

'Felix wants me to do some more paintings for him. And he is going to pay me for each one. Can you believe it?'

'Oh Shaky, that is tremendous news,' said PC. 'You are the best. I'm glad I took a photo of *The Chimeras*. I look at it all the time.'

'I will pay for your dance classes from now on PC, and Teabag's medical school fees, and Sly's cooking classes, and everything for everyone.'

'Calm down. Just paint, and we will see what happens. When do you start?'

'Now. Felix is going to send me some supplies, and as soon as they come, I'll start.'

'What's your first one?'

'I've got a list. The first is going to be the *Girl with a Pearl Earring*, I think. He says he has buyers for all of them already.'

'I will pose for you. I have a pearl earring,' said PC.

'He said it has to be like the original. So no cats, I'm afraid.'

'Okay. Shame though,' said PC, disappointed.

oOo

At dinner, Sly produced Shaky's favourite pudding, with creamy custard, by way of a celebration.

Suddenly there was a loud knock on the front door.

Grandad went to open it. There, on the doorstep, stood two burly cats holding crates. There were more crates beside them on the ground.

'Special delivery for Shaky,' one delivery cat said.

'This way, this way,' said Grandad, surprised at the number of materials.

There were canvases, paints, palettes, brushes, pencils, charcoal, turpentine, cloths, aprons and two easels.

'You will have to use my den for the time being,' said Grandad to Shaky who had followed behind the delivery cats.

'Wow, thank you, Grandad. Are you sure?'

'You could earn a lot of money. You are going to need quiet, and there is an awful lot of stuff. That Felix is very generous.'

When the delivery cats had left, Shaky went back to his pudding, licking his lips and wiping over his face with his paw to get every last drop.

'Talk about the cat that got the cream,' said Sly, sarcastically.

'Literally,' laughed Teddy.

o0o

Every day after school Shaky got to work. He found a picture of the *Girl with a Pearl Earring* online. Shaky made sure he prepared the colours he would need beforehand. He donned one of the aprons that had been delivered, tying the straps loosely around his waist. The two easels meant that he could start another painting while he was waiting for the first one to dry. It was a challenge to alter his usual style, but it was a useful exercise. He would discover what he liked best. He did not usually paint in oils, although *The Chimeras* was in oils.

Shaky finished the *Girl with a Pearl Earring* and had an idea for the painting to make it more spectacular, and with a final flourish of his brush, he was done. Perfect, he thought, pleased. When the picture seemed dry enough, he draped the easel with a dust sheet.

Now to the next. Shaky had already started on Vincent van Gogh's *Sunflowers*. Again, he was careful about the various shades of yellow for the flowers, the wonky vase and the yellow background. Lots of yellow.

oOo

Everyone was asleep when suddenly, there was banging on the front door. It was two panther-like cats, large and menacing. They slinked into the house before being invited in, demanding the paintings that Shaky had completed. There was another panther-like cat who did not come into the house; he seemed to be keeping watch.

'Why can't they come at a decent hour?' tutted Mummy Cat, her hair in rollers. 'The kittens have school in the morning.'

Teabag was up, still studying when she heard the noise outside and plugged in her headphones to listen to a podcast about pandemics.

'Who are the buyers?' asked Shaky.

'Never you mind,' grunted the burliest Panther. 'We have to get these to the boat.'

'Where are they going?' enquired Shaky, not one bit surprised when the Panther growled, 'Never you mind.'

By then nearly all the kittens, including Grandad, were in the den watching the Panthers start to secure the two paintings in bubble-wrap and cloth.

'Wait!' shouted PC. 'I have to take a picture.'

Irritated, the Panthers placed the paintings in separate crates and nailed the boxes shut, but PC had her pictures. After putting a label on each container, finally, they left, but not before saying, 'We will be back for the others next week. Have all of them done by then, or Felix will not be happy. We have buyers.'

The Panther waiting outside came in and gave Shaky a large envelope.

Shaky gave the envelope to Grandad.

'I don't like them,' said Teddy. 'Not one bit.'

'This might change your mind, kitty cat,' said Grandad who was peeking at the contents of the envelope. 'This looks like ten thousand pounds.'

oOo

Shaky worked furiously on new paintings. *The Scream* first, and the *Mona Lisa* next. The *Mona Lisa* was smaller than he'd expected, and he made sure that it was the exact same size as the original. When he finished his work, he stacked the paintings against the wall behind Grandad's armchair, so that they would not be in the way. Shaky loved his interpretations of these masterpieces. The final stroke of his paintbrush heralded the completion. Now Shaky was not only dressed in an apron; he had perched on his head a black beret. He was an artist and looked like one. Grandad had told him about Dilts' Neurological Levels.

Grandad said something about having a suitable and conducive environment to be who you wanted to be. Grandad's den was now his studio, check. Shaky made a tick in the air with his paintbrush. A blob of paint splattered onto the wall. 'Behaviour. I paint. You can't be an artist if you don't paint. Check.' Shaky drew a tinier invisible tick in the air with his paintbrush so as not to make a mess. 'Skills and knowledge, check. I know how to paint. Values and beliefs?' He thought about this. 'Yes, I believe in myself. Check.' Everyone else thought he was a very talented artist, and so did Felix. 'Identity? Who am I? I am Shaky the artist. Check. And what impact will I have on the world? I am selling my work for a shedload of money, and I can help my family, so my paintings will be my legacy. Check, check, check,' said Shaky, out loud, satisfied with himself.

oOo

The Panthers came back a week later for *The Scream* and *Mona Lisa*. PC had already taken photos because she did not want to make them angry. Again, the artwork was wrapped up carefully in bubble wrap and thick blankets. The Panthers nailed the crates shut and put labels on each one—ML for *Mona Lisa* and TS for *The Scream.*

The Panthers gave Shaky another envelope full of cash, and they told Shaky gruffly that they would be back for the rest in two weeks. Shaky was relieved that he had an extra week, but he still had to work hard to get them completed in time.

'I am not sure I can do them in two weeks,' said Shaky boldly.

The biggest Panther looked at him sternly. Shaky gulped and added weakly, 'But I will do my best.'

The Panthers went out, slamming the door so hard that the house shook.

Two weeks went by so quickly, but Shaky managed to paint Andy Warhol's *Soup* picture, then he had a go at David Hockney's *Mr and Mrs Clark.* A lot was going on in the Hockney picture because it was the scene of a living room and somewhat cluttered.

'That's it,' said Shaky to no one in particular. 'I'm done. I hope I don't hear from Felix any time soon. Painting is not fun when you have to do it to such a tight deadline, and it isn't your choice of subject. But I did enjoy the challenge.'

'When are they coming to collect the paintings, Shaky?' asked PC, snapping them all with her polaroid camera.

'Today, or tomorrow,' said Shaky. 'I have lost track of time. It would be good to get my life back.'

'To do what? asked PC.

'Paint. But what *I* want to paint.'

oOo

It was unnerving waiting for the Panthers to turn up, but eventually, they did. They went about protecting the artwork meticulously, gave Shaky an envelope full of cash and drove off, screeching their car tyres when they rounded the corner, just missing a removal van coming into the street.

CHAPTER EIGHT

The New Neighbours

The whole family were on the doorstep, almost as if to make sure that the panther-looking cats were gone.

The van stopped across the road.

'More removal cats,' sighed Mummy Cat.

'Looks like a family is moving in,' said Teddy. 'I hope they're nice.'

'A big family, by the look of the amount of furniture they have. Oh, I love that sofa. Love the colour. Looks cosy,' said Teddy.

'Let's go in, I am sure they don't want nosy neighbours watching them,' said Mummy Cat.

'I'll make a cake and welcome them to the street,' suggested Sly.

'That is a lovely idea, Sly,' said Mummy Cat

When the cake cooled and the icing had hardened, Teddy and Sly wrapped it in a clean tea cloth, put the cake in a tin, and crossed the road to the new household. There was still furniture on the front lawn. They could hear music inside and the sound of arguing.

'Oh dear, should we come back later?' suggested Teddy.

'We are just dropping it off, and saying hello,' said Sly pressing the bell and knocking on the door for good measure.

Suddenly the door opened. A large cat stood swaying at the door, burping loudly. The cat was still in pyjamas and slippers.

'Yes?' he slurred.

'We live across the road,' said Sly. 'We made you a cake to welcome you to the street.'

The cat looked at the kittens, took the cake and slammed the door.

'Well, how rude!' said Teddy. 'We are going to have neighbours that we hate, and we have to see them every day.'

'I am going to ask for my tin back,' said Sly, banging on the door.

This time a good-looking young kitten opened the door.

'Hello,' he said. 'Did you bring over that cake?'

'Yes. Coffee and walnut. And I want my tin back,' said Sly, huffily. 'That cat who opened the door was insulting. He didn't even say thank you, or no thank you. I want my tin back.'

'Hold on a sec,' said the kitten. He disappeared into the house and emerged a few moments later with the empty cake tin and the tea towel.

'I am sorry about my dad's behaviour. He's stressed because of all the moving. Half of our furniture has not arrived, and the removal company has smashed all our plates and mugs.'

'Your dad's probably drunk by the look of him and smashed the plates himself. But that's still no excuse to be so rude,' said Sly sharply.

'I know, I know. You don't choose your parents, do you? You get what you get. He's my stepdad anyway, and we all hate him,' said the kitten lowering his voice in case the stepdad was nearby.

'What's your name' enquired Teddy feeling a bit sorry for him. 'I'm Teddy, and this is my twin brother, Sly.'

'I'm Stuart Havana-Brown.'

'Hello Stuart Havana-Brown,' said Sly, emphasising the pronunciation of each syllable in a sarcastic manner.

'You can come over if you like. Get out of your stepdad's way. Meet our family,' offered Teddy, giving Sly a look.

'I'll just check with my mum.'

Stuart disappeared into the darkness of the house once more. This time he emerged wearing a jacket. 'Mum said thank you for the cake, and that I mustn't be too long.'

Stuart closed the door behind him and followed the twins across the road.

Grandad was in his den reading the papers. Mummy Cat was in the utility room, doing the laundry. Teabag was studying in her bedroom, and PC was in the living room with Milo, practising a jive dance routine to the song *Pata Pata* by Miriam Makeba. Shaky was sketching them quietly in the corner of the room, glancing at PC and Milo from time to time, quite impressed at the way she was able to break down the dance steps patiently so that Milo could follow, but he was not getting it.

'I can only do the Latin dances, PC. Jive is not my thing.'

'I'm back to square one, with no dance partner, again,' said PC, more sharply than she intended.

'I'm going to see Scooter, anyway. He has a new video game, and then we are going to play football out the back,' retorted Milo, quite frustrated and tired.

'Who is this?' asked PC, spying Stuart behind the twins at the living room door.

'Oh, this is Stuart Havana-Brown, our new neighbour,' said Teddy.

'Did you like the cake?' asked PC. 'Sly made it especially for you.'

'Yes, that was very kind. What dances do you do?' asked Stuart.

'Milo and I do Latin,' said PC, pointing to Milo. 'But, I have to do loads of different styles, and I am going to need a new partner.'

It was then that Stuart realised that Milo was a dog. He arched his back.

'What is wrong with you lot? Do what you like in your own home, but in mine, you have to be polite.'

'I'm sorry,' said Stuart. 'I can hip-hop and breakdance.'

'Really?' said PC, smiling.

'It's not okay him being rude to me, just because he can dance,' said Milo haughtily.

'He did apologise,' reasoned PC.

'Oh, that's alright then,' said Milo, taking off his headband and throwing it on the floor, before storming off to find Scooter.

'What a prima donna,' said PC, tying the headband around her neck.

'Oi, I heard that,' said Milo from the hall.

The kittens giggled, but they felt bad for being mean to Milo.

oOo

'What's up, Milo?' said Scooter, looking into his friend's face.

'PC's got a new dance partner. I don't think I should come here anymore,' said Milo sadly.

'That's a bit drastic,' said Scooter, surprised and shocked. 'Should I have a word with her?'

'No!'

Scooter went to get a drink from the kitchen. He got one for Milo too, but when he got back to his room, Milo was gone.

Scooter raced to the living room. 'What did you say to Milo?' Scooter demanded.

'We didn't say anything,' said PC. 'He just got the hump.'

'Well he's gone, and he is never coming back. Thanks a lot.'

Scooter furrowed his brow in sorrow. Milo was his best friend.

'We are sorry,' said Teddy. 'Should we go to his house and talk to him?'

'Let him cool off a bit and then talk to him,' said Stuart.

'Who's this?' asked Scooter.

'Stuart Havana-Brown, from across the road,' said Sly.

'We can't be mean to our friends,' said Scooter, leaving the room. 'I'm going to go and find him.'

'I'll come with you,' said Teddy.

'Me too,' said Sly.

'Er, I'm going home,' said Stuart. 'Thank you for the cake.'

'What a messed up day this has turned out to be,' said PC, sitting down next to Shaky, adjusting Milo's headband around her slender neck.

oOo

Scooter thought he would be quicker on his own and told the twins not to come. It was getting dark anyway.

He ran to the park quickly. He saw a little speck of white near the gate at the other end of the park. That was Milo, walking slowly, his head bowed. Scooter tried calling, but Milo couldn't hear him from the distance between them.

Scooter realised that he did not know where Milo lived, so he continued to follow him. At one point, Milo stopped and looked around. Something made Scooter slink behind a tree.

Out of the park, Milo turned right and carried on walking for some time. He passed all the houses on the street until he came to what appeared to be a dead end. Scooter saw a wide metal gate that cut across a path leading to a recreational ground. There was a skate park up ahead and a clearing. Milo climbed through the gate and then ran into the bushes by the entrance.

Scooter followed hesitantly, hidden by some branches. There he saw a little tent camouflaged among some fallen tree trunks and bushes. In front, attached to two tree branches was a clothesline made of old string, from which hung a t-shirt and four little boots. The boots that Teddy had given Milo for Christmas. Scooter backed away and ran all the way home.

oOo

Scooter went straight to Grandad's den.

'What is it, Scooter?' asked Grandad, concerned. 'You seem upset.'

'I think Milo's sleeping rough.'

'How do you know?' asked Grandad.

'He left here after having a row with PC, and I followed him, to cheer him up, to talk to him. He went to the recreation ground.'

'Are you sure?'

'Yes. I followed.'

'He didn't go into a house, Milo's got a tent,' said Scooter. 'He's sleeping in the bushes.'

'That's terrible,' said Grandad, sadly. 'I wonder what has happened to his family. He's alone.'

'And it's dangerous.'

'You didn't talk to him?' asked Grandad.

'No. I think Milo would be embarrassed for me to see him like that. Oh Grandad, what are we going to do?' asked Scooter.

'Shelter, food and security are the basic needs of all creatures as much as the need to breathe and sleep are. Let's go and get him,' said Grandad kindly. 'He can stay with us.'

With that, Scooter and Grandad went to find Milo. Scooter led the way.

When they got to the recreational ground, Scooter picked his way through the fallen branches and bushes to the spot where he last saw Milo.

'The tent's gone. Milo's not here!' he exclaimed.

'Are you sure this is the place?' asked Grandad.

Scooter wasn't sure. Then he saw the clothesline. It was still up, but everything that was hanging on it had gone.

Milo had disappeared.

CHAPTER NINE

We Watch TikTok Too!

It was the Easter holiday break from school. Two whole weeks. The weather was cold and wet so no going out to play. That suited Sly, who lazily snuggled down in bed most days. All the kittens were bored and slept most of the time, only emerging to eat. Today they were in the living room playing board games. Grandad was reading, and Mummy Cat was ironing. Sly had cooked buffets most days, so everyone could help themselves whenever they wanted. Grandad tried to muster some enthusiasm. 'You kitty cats have plenty to do. You have homework, and you will have exams when you get back. The only one doing any real work is Teabag.'

'I am doing some research,' said Scooter. 'And I am still looking for Milo. No one has seen him or heard from him. I'm worried.'

'I am experimenting with different art styles,' said Shaky. 'And I want to visit some art museums next week. Anyone want to come?'

'No!' chorused all the kittens at the same time.

'Suit yourselves,' said Shaky, slightly put out. No one was remotely interested in his work. Maybe PC, a little. His family always said his artwork was good, but without any real appreciation of art, what was their opinion worth? Nothing, he concluded.

'You never heard from that Felix, the art dealer again, did you? You never did meet him, did you?' asked Grandad, peeping up from his newspaper.

'Only spoke to him on the phone that one time,' said Shaky. 'I would work for him again. It was hard but interesting, and we have all that money.'

'What did he sound like?' asked Grandad.

'Not sure. Felix just said what he wanted me to do and that was it. I did it, and those scary Panthers collected the paintings. Hard to tell on the phone. Seemed okay.'

'I am going to see if Stuart wants to work on a dance routine,' said PC, biting on a crunchy fish-flavoured biscuit.

'I can make new costumes if you like,' offered Teddy.

'Thanks, Teddy, but I don't know what routine I will be doing yet. It's not the same without Milo. He was such a great salsa dancer. And bachata. And rhumba. Anything Latino. I miss him.'

'We all do,' said Scooter, more sharply than he intended.

'I am going to make some hot cross buns. And it is a fish pie for lunch,' said Sly, hoping that a good meal would cheer everyone up.

'What's for the topping, pastry or potatoes?' asked Teddy.

'More fish,' said Sly. 'We don't need the carbs.'

'What are you going to do, Grandad?' asked Scooter.

'Now that you are all occupied, I'll listen to some music, I think. Anything I can help you with Scoots? You said you were doing some research.'

'Not sure. I am investigating social media platforms and some technical stuff. I'm listening to a load of podcasts to see what's out there and YouTube stuff.'

'You know, in my day we went to the library to get our information, but now, you can learn everything online.'

'I don't know why we have to go to school anymore. We can learn everything we need on our laptops. You could even read the papers online, Grandad.'

'I like the feel of a newspaper. School is not just for lessons, you know. It is about building lifelong friendships with different people, learning to get on with others. Sport. Structure. Critical thinking. Preparing for a career,' said Grandad thoughtfully.

'More like being a cog in a great big machine,' offered Scooter.

'I have to admit it feels like that, sometimes,' agreed Grandad. 'The world is changing. Work is not a regular place to go to anymore for many. Cats work from home on Zoom, a coffee shop, a library or even a park bench.'

'We are still factory fodder, and there are no more factories. They don't teach us to set up businesses. I think all of us in this house will do our own thing, except Teabag. And she is the most stressed. Too stressed to eat even,' said Teddy.

'Yes, she missed breakfast this morning,' added Sly.

'That's okay,' said Scooter. 'I had her share, so no worries.'

'Well, I brought her a snack. She ate that,' said Sly.

'No, I had that too,' said Scooter. 'So, no waste there either.'

'Good, I don't like wasting food. Not my delicious snacks anyway,' said Sly.

'Should we invite our new neighbours over?' asked PC.

'No,' said Sly, at once.

'Stuart is okay,' said Teddy. 'The stepdad is always drunk. I've seen him. And the little ones are at nursery most of the time.'

'What about the mother?' asked Mummy Cat. 'I would have liked a new friend to gossip with, but she seems standoffish. Just tired, I expect. She goes off to work early in the morning and comes back late. It's Stuart who looks after his siblings. He's good with them. He has a lot on his plate.'

'Not as much as greedy Scooter, eating all of Teabag's meals.'

'Ho ho ho,' said Scooter, holding his belly in mock mirth.

'Well, let's invite Stuart over for lunch. If he is helping PC with a new routine, I dare say he will be here at lunchtime anyway,' said Grandad.

o0o

Grandad went to find Teabag. She had missed both dinner the previous evening and breakfast.

'How's studying going?'

'It's not,' said Teabag sharply.

'Oh?' said Grandad.

'I am writing loads of notes, and nothing is sinking in. I need straight As if I have any hope of getting into med school,' said Teabag. 'It's so frustrating.'

Grandad raised an eyebrow. 'Writing notes is not the most efficient way of studying.'

'What do you mean?' asked Teabag.

'Mind maps. They resemble brain cells, and they connect one piece of information to another. It reduces the need for remembering, and encourages knowing. You can reduce a whole textbook to just one huge mind map.'

'I don't understand,' said Teabag, perplexed.

'Put your main point in the middle of your page, then draw branches of subheadings off from it. Like a spider almost. Then as you understand more and find out new things, you add to your diagram. Use different colours for each branch. Shaky can let you have some colours, I'm sure. Draw pictures and symbols that make sense to you. No need for lots of notes. Create a picture.'

'I see. I have heard of mind maps, but I didn't think they worked.'

'It is hard to let go of the old habit of taking notes, but the brain does not work linearly. Also, if you have new information, you have to write your notes out all over again. This way, if you have new information, you just add another branch.'

'That makes sense,' said Teabag thoughtfully.

'You know, if you have to write an essay, you can picture your mind map, and you can easily "see" the points that you want to make.'

'You make studying seem so easy.'

'There are two more points to take into account,' added Grandad. 'Number one: study for around forty-five minutes at a time.'

'But I've got loads to do, Grandad,' wailed Teabag.

'I know. Therefore, you have to be efficient. Study for that amount of time, then do something completely different. You remember best the first thing you study. It's called the primacy effect. You will also remember the last thing you studied. That's called the recency effect. So, it makes sense to reduce the time in the middle. And point number two: before you start studying again, review your work.' Grandad emphasized the word "review." 'Review what you are learning to make sure you understand it. That means you look over your mind map because it is a picture. Anything you don't understand, or have forgotten, look it up. Add more information that comes up for you and make the connections.'

'I will give it a go, Grandad,' said Teabag sceptically.

'You're not convinced, are you? You have had a lifetime of studying by writing notes and using flashcards. Try mind maps. My friend Tony has helped so many to learn how to study. Millions cannot be wrong.'

'Okay, Grandad,' said Teabag, a bit more enthusiastically.

'Good kitty cat,' said Grandad, ruffling her hair.

Teabag frowned.

'You will always be my kitty cat, no matter how big you get.'

Teabag couldn't help smiling. 'Love you, Grandad.'

oOo

Stuart came over for lunch. Fish pie, with fish topping, yum; and to dance with PC.

'Let's start the routine first, Stuart. Lunch is not ready yet. What's that?' asked PC, pointing to Stuart's head.

'What?' said Stuart.

'Your eye. Bloodshot. And you have a torn ear,' said PC, shocked.

'Oh. Oh, it's nothing. It doesn't hurt. Not any more,' said Stuart, touching his ear gingerly.

'So, how did you get a black eye then?' asked PC, front paws on hips.

'I fell,' said Stuart.

'Kittens don't fall. We always land on all fours.'

'I banged into something,' offered Stuart unconvincingly.

'Yeah. You banged into your stepdad's claws, repeatedly, I expect.'

Stuart laughed, but the laughter did not reach his beautiful green eyes.

'Is it that obvious? When I get bigger, I'd like to smack him, but I don't want to be like him. No way,' said Stuart, with determination.

'I am so sorry,' said PC. 'It can't be fun living in fear.'

'I like coming here. You lot get on with each other,' said Stuart enviously.

'Not all the time, but we don't argue for long, and we certainly don't fight. And we all love each other.'

'Dancing helps me to forget,' said Stuart wistfully. 'Thanks to you.'

'Dancing is everything to me,' said PC.

PC pressed play, and the opening bars of 'Jerusalema' came on by Master KG. They both started tapping their right paws four times, then their left paws four times, then shuffled all their legs, losing themselves in the music.

'You know you are supposed to dance to this with a plate of food in your paw,' said Stuart. 'I've seen loads of videos of this song and the dance routine.'

'Yes. It's funny. You're sitting down to a meal, but the rhythm grabs you so much, you have to dance,' agreed PC, clenching and opening her claws.

oOo

'Lunch,' shouted Sly.

PC and Stuart ran into the kitchen giggling. PC had brought in her music player and pressed play. These words rang out.

> *Jerusalema ikahaya lami*
> *Ngilondoloze*
> *Uhambe nami*
> *Zungangishiyi Lana*

To her and Stuart's astonishment, Grandad, Mummy Cat and all the kittens stood up, plates in paw and started to dance the *Jerusalema* routine.

'We watch TikTok too, kitty cat,' said Grandad with a wink, before dipping down, turning, and dancing in unison with the rest of the family.

CHAPTER TEN

And Cut!

'I want to start a YouTube channel,' said Scooter one morning. 'I'm going to call it *The Scooter Show.*'

'Why *The Scooter Show*? Why not the PC Show?' asked PC, chewing on a piece of toast.

'Or the Teddy and Sly Show?' asked Sly, helping himself to more jam.

'Hey, this is my idea and my show,' said Scooter indignantly. 'You will be my guests. It's going to be a kind of keeping up with the kittens, only better. I'll write an outline for it. And you can tell me what you think.'

'Seems like you've made up your mind,' sulked Sly.

'Hey, YouTube is available to everyone. You can start a show if you want. Nothing is stopping you. I have the technical know-how, and I have the camera, the microphone, the green screen. And I am getting new lighting.' Scooter felt he was too defensive. He wanted encouragement, not obstacles.

None of the kittens knew what a green screen was, so they gave up arguing.

'Where are you going to put all that stuff for the recording?' asked Teabag, concerned, drinking a glass of water and pushing away her barely touched oatmeal.

'Grandad said I could use his den,' said Scooter matter-of-factly. 'He let Shaky use it for his painting, so he will let me use it when I need to.'

'So with Shaky painting in there and now you, where is Grandad going to read his papers?' asked Mummy Cat.

'Oh I can go into the living room or the kitchen,' said Grandad.

'PC's in the living room, dancing, and Sly's in the kitchen, cooking,' said Mummy Cat.

'I use my bedroom floor for my dressmaking,' said Teddy smugly.

'Our bedroom,' corrected Sly.

'Maybe I could use the garden shed, although Shaky uses it too, sometimes. No, I am happy for everyone to use the space we have for activities. The den was great to have while you were tiny because I could get some peace and quiet, but now you are all at school, I have the daytime all to myself, so I'm okay. What's *The Scooter Show* going to be about?'

'Well, I thought that it would be a variety show. I will do a funny take on the news. Then Teddy will tell us where the bargains are and how to customise and recycle old clothes. PC can do a dance routine. Teabag can tell us about how to keep fit and about healthy eating, and Sly can cook a dish.'

'That sounds like it could be entertaining. Any role for me?' asked Grandad.

'Or me?' asked Mummy Cat.

'Er, no,' said Scooter, embarrassed. 'The show is for kittens, by kittens.'

'Ageism,' retorted Grandad, smiling. 'Well. We will be on hand to offer support and to fact check any historical events, since we are so old and useless.'

'Thanks, Grandad,' said Scooter, ignoring his sarcasm. He added quickly, 'I want to put a show out every week. The first show will be next week. I will record on Sunday. Rehearsal on Saturday and a meeting on Tuesday after school, to go through the programme.'

'Scooter's strict. If he gets all bossy, I will tell him where to shove his YouTube video,' Sly whispered to Teddy.

'It's a good idea, actually,' conceded Teddy. 'I will see you one at a time for the meetings, so you'd better have your plan. Then on rehearsal day, you rehearse and refine your slot, and on Sunday, I record. I will do some editing, add music and link the slots together into one great programme.'

'Scooter seems to know what he wants. See,' said Teddy. 'He only wants us to do our best. And if we look good, he looks good.'

Sly frowned, not yet convinced.

oOo

Scooter sat in Grandad's armchair in the den. He sent a text to Teddy.

Your meeting is in five minutes.
Come to the den with
your best ideas. Scoot.

'I'm so nervous. What is Scooter going to say to me?' asked Teddy when she received the text message.

'You have to do the talking, Teddy. You have to tell him what you are going to do and how long it is going to take. And if you need anything,' said Sly, also wondering what he was going to cook first. Sly made up his mind that he was not going to let Scooter boss him around. He would cook what he wanted to cook.

Teddy went to the den and knocked softly on the door.

'Come in, Teddy,' Scooter shouted from inside. Scooter thought he would leave the door open next time. He did not want to intimidate his siblings, but he also wanted them to take him and *The Scooter Show* seriously.

'So tell me what you've got planned?'

Scooter was wearing a shirt and tie, which made him look immensely grown-up and very professional.

'Well,' said Teddy, clearing her throat, 'I am going to, I mean, I want to showcase how I create new designs by customizing old clothes. I have made them unique and beyond fashion. I can do that every time.'

'Have you got a name for your segment?' enquired Scooter, smiling at Teddy, who seemed nervous to him.

'No. Not yet.' And then Teddy's eyes lit up. 'I want it to be called *Teddy's Beyond Fashion Slot.* I need ten minutes. And I want people to send in pictures of their work too. Also, I have made all of PC's dance costumes, so I want PC to model all her outfits at some point.'

'That sounds perfect, Teddy. You have thought about this. I am going to give you five minutes because we will film the relevant stages of your work. We don't have to show every single stitch; you know what I mean. It's called editing.'

'Oh I see.'

'I will have to film your work, and then cut out the bits we don't need. We will call your slot *Beyond Fashion, by Teddy*.'

'Okay.' Teddy grinned and could not help bouncing up and down on her four paws. She stopped when she saw Scooter staring at her, bemused. 'Too much?'

'Can you call in PC now? I want to hear what she has planned. Leave the door open, thanks,' said Scooter, dismissing Teddy.

Teddy was excited. She allowed herself to punch the air with a paw. *'Beyond Fashion, by Teddy*. 'You are next, PC. You'd better come up with something good.'

'I have, don't worry about me.'

oOo

'Hello, PC. Take a seat', said Scooter, smiling.

'You know this is for you to showcase your talent?'

'Yes. It's a great opportunity.'

'So what have you come up with?'

'I am going to do a dance routine every week, and then I am going to break it down into basic steps for kittens to follow. So, for this week I am going to do a jive to 'Sha Boom' by the Chords, a Doo-Wop band from the nineteen fifties. I would jive to a much faster song, but I want viewers to notice the flicks and the kicks. It's a nice song too.'

'So you will be showcasing different styles of dances and then teaching some basic steps?'

'Yes.'

'So, you will have five minutes.'

'I am going to need more time.'

'No. Five is what I am giving you.'

'What if people don't get the steps?'

'Then they can watch the video again. And again, and again.'

'Mmm, that's true. Okay.'

'Yes, PC. I want *The Scooter Show* to be snappy. No long pauses. Thank you, PC. I look forward to your slot. How would you like to be introduced?'

'*Dancing with PC?*'

'Perfect. Can you get Sly for me?'

'Yeah, sure.' PC breathed a sigh of relief.

o0o

Sly was waiting outside the door. PC nearly smashed into him.

'How is Attila the Hun?'

'It's okay. Go in.'

Sly entered sheepishly. 'Okay, Scoot?'

'PC and Teddy are doing what they do best. And you, what's your plan?'

'My bit is going to be about cooking. If you are filming on Sunday, you can film me making the Sunday dinner or the pudding bit.'

'Not a roast every time?' Scooter frowned.

'No, I will cook something different and delicious each week. And, what's more, we get to eat it after.'

'Win, win. You have to prepare everything beforehand. All the ingredients. To save on time.'

'No problem. You'll just film the stages. We don't have to show me peeling every potato and slicing every carrot.' Sly had watched lots of TV cookery shows.

'Indeed,' said Scooter.

'You sound like Grandad,' said Sly.

'Thanks,' said Scooter, not sure if Sly meant it as a compliment. Knowing Sly, it was not. 'Well I did have a conversation with Grandad about time management, so that is why I am doing this. I had a look at the time I spent doing different things every day and found that I was wasting a lot of it. Out of one hundred and sixty-eight hours a week, I spent a lot of time doing nothing in particular. By being a bit more organised, I can do something more constructive, like this YouTube show. And everyone can showcase their skills.'

'Sure,' said Sly, rolling his eyes.

Scooter noticed. 'If the video is no good, we don't have to upload it. And if we get fed up, we will stop.'

'Okay. I'm in. For the first show, I am going to keep it simple and make a coconut and lime cake. Or a pie. I haven't decided which yet.'

'We can film everything you cook and put the clips out when we want. And you know what is nice?' said Scooter grinning.

'What?' asked Sly.

'Us eating the food afterwards.'

'Yeah, that is the nice part.'

o0o

Scooter sent for Teabag.

Teabag was quite excited but apprehensive.

'I don't know how I can contribute. I have nothing to offer. I have no practical skills like Shaky, Sly or Teddy. By the way, Shaky said he is not going to do anything. He's not coming to a meeting with you.'

'Fair enough,' said Scooter. He thought he would be able to showcase Shaky's work anyway. 'Let's make a list of what you can do, Tea, and see what comes up. I have some ideas.'

'What ideas? Let's hear them then.'

'Okay. I think you can talk about health and fitness, as we said before. You know, diets. Eating the right food. Exercise.'

Teabag looked doubtful. 'The TV and the papers are always ramming that down our necks. It's boring.'

'What about giving advice? Kittens can write in, and you can tell them what they should do.'

'What if no one writes in?'

'We can make up some problems.'

'Won't that be cheating?'

Scooter was becoming frustrated with Teabag's attitude and lack of enthusiasm. 'A few, just so everyone gets the idea, and then new subscribers will start to send in their problems. We will write about the concerns that every kitten has.'

'Maybe,' said Teabag doubtfully.

'What about this for a problem, "Dear Teabag, I have a sister who is a right pain when trying to come up with an idea for my YouTube show".'

'Look Scooter, I don't know if I can do this. I'm camera shy as well, and I don't have an angle.'

'Out of all of us, Teabag, I thought you would be right on it.'

Teabag hung her head. It was quite a thing for her younger brother to be disappointed in her.

Scooter was surprised to see that Teabag didn't have any confidence or self-assurance. She hid behind her books the whole time. Scooter was at a loss.

Teabag sat, staring at the floor.

'Okay,' she said, sighing.

Scooter believed she was going to refuse to be part of *The Scooter Show*. It would be a shame if Teabag were not in it.

'Okay,' said Scooter. He could find no words. He was thinking in his mind that he would give each of his siblings a little more time. They wanted more time anyway.

'I will ask Teddy, Sly and PC, even Stuart from across the road to come up a problem. That way they won't be fake, and then I will give advice as best I can. I just want one problem each time because I want to research the best response. I need five minutes. And my slot should be called, um, *Teabag's Advice Corner*, because I will sit in the corner of the living room.'

'That's brilliant', Scooter said thoughtfully. 'I think your slot is going to be the most important of all the slots. You'll see.'

Scooter had filmed almost all the sections of *The Scooter Show*. As planned, they were eating the meal that Sly had cooked. None of the family had to pretend to like the food. It was delicious. But, because of the filming, the conversation was stilted, and they laughed too loudly, and for too long.

'Listen up. Relax. I'm not going to film anymore,' Scooter said, thinking that none of the show should go unrehearsed, even eating a meal around the table. Talking and eating proved difficult. 'I'll just use some music when we are eating, that's it. This part is only a few moments anyway.'

Relieved, the family started to act naturally. There was the usual banter that was genuinely funny.

'Oh Scooter you should have kept the camera on. This was great, and you missed it,' said Teddy.

'No I didn't miss anything,' said Scooter, winking. 'I kept the tape rolling, as they say. I got everything.'

CHAPTER ELEVEN

The Prank

Dinner was over, and after everyone had helped with the clearing up, it was Teabag's turn to be filmed by Scooter. After seeing what everyone else had done, Teabag was a little less anxious.

Teabag chose to sit in Grandad's den for her bit, not the living room, after all. Everyone had sent in a problem. Teabag picked one at random. She was dressed very elegantly and seemed more confident than she felt.

'We can edit out the bits you don't like, even reshoot the whole thing, Teabag. Just relax. Be yourself,' said Scooter reassuringly.

'Hello everyone. My name is Teabag, and this is Teabag's Advice Corner. Each week, please send me your problem, and I will try my best to give you some good advice. All names will remain confidential. Here is the first letter, and it's from Stuart.'

She stopped abruptly. Teabag had given out the name of the writer of the letter after promising not to.

'Carry on,' said Scooter. 'I can edit that out.'

Teabag carried on. 'Here is the first letter from S. It says *My name is Stuart*.' Teabag stopped again.

Scooter circled his paw in the air, a sign for her to carry on.

'Have you got a marker pen?' asked Teabag, not trusting herself not to repeat Stuart's name.

Teabag blocked out every occurrence of Stuart's name and other names in the letter. She wrote in the initials over the blocked-out words.

'Okay. Let's go, one more time,' said Scooter encouragingly.

'I have a letter here from S. He says this: *My mum married again after my dad died. I don't get on with my stepdad. When T is drunk, he takes it out on me. He has sharp claws. I hate being at home sometimes because he is always snarling at us. We are scared of him. I can't wait to leave home, but I won't because I need to protect my brothers and sisters.*

'Thank you for sending me this letter, S. First of all; no one should have to live like this, experiencing physical and emotional abuse.'

Teabag looked straight at the camera.

'You don't mention if you have spoken to your mother. I am sure she would not be happy if she knew how you felt. Furthermore, you say you are protecting your siblings. Again, no kitten should have to be in that position. Being a kitten is a time for play and having fun. I would strongly advise calling the RSPCK. The Royal Society for the Prevention of Cruelty to Kittens.

'The number is on your screen below. However, I did call them on your behalf, S. They want you to get in touch with them, and they will support you.

'Please talk to your mother or a teacher or a grownup you trust as well.'

Smiling now, Teabag said, 'Thank you, S. Please let us know how you get on.

'That's it from *Teabag's Advice Corner*. See you next time.'

Scooter could not help clapping. 'That was brilliant, Teabag. Good. And who knew that about Stuart?'

oOo

One afternoon Sly and Teddy were in the kitchen, making a snack for everyone. Whitebait sandwiches, cheese, melon, and milk. They were going to watch their favourite film, *A Street Cat Named Bob*.

'I love Bob,' said PC.

'I prefer Keanu, the gangster kitten. He's my favourite,' said Teddy.

The Easter break was more exciting now that they had *The Scooter Show* to record, and this was a moment to relax. Stuart seemed always to be around and was becoming part of their family. He hadn't made up his mind about calling the RSPCK, but he was grateful that he had somewhere else to go and kittens who understood what he was going through.

Sly took the fish out of the fridge and some vegetables and when bringing them over to the table dropped the cucumber.

'Oops,' said Sly.

Just then PC came in to see what was taking so long. Seeing what looked like a green snake from the corner of her eye, PC leapt three feet into the air, smashing into the dustbin and sending it flying.

Scooter ran in to see what the noise was, and he too jumped up when he saw what he believed to be a snake.

Teddy and Sly were doubled up in laughter, snorting loudly.

'Oh, oh my tummy hurts,' said Sly, tears streaming down his face. 'It's a cucumber, dummies. Your faces. Oh, oh, oh.'

'Those sandwiches had better be good,' said PC haughtily, leaving the kitchen, tail straight and high.

'That PC never had a sense of humour,' said Scooter. 'You can stop laughing now, twins, but I must admit, it was funny.'

PC returned to the kitchen with Stuart. 'Can Stuart help you?' PC winked at her siblings.

'Yes,' said Sly. 'Stuart, could you pick that up off the floor?'

'Ahhhh!' Stuart cried, seeing the cucumber for the first time. He too did a leap and a skip to get away from it as fast as he could, bashing into Scooter.

'It's a cucumber Stuart,' said Scooter. 'The twins pranked us.'

'Why does that happen? It is so obviously a cucumber when you look at it,' said Stuart, relieved, even though he'd never seen a snake before.

'That's the point,' said Scooter. 'We don't stop to think. We convince ourselves unconsciously that it is a snake and try to get away as quickly as possible. It's our survival instinct.'

'Isn't that a good thing?' asked Teddy.

'Of course. There aren't any snakes around here. But if there were, we would get out of harm's way, quickly.'

'Teddy. Sly. Can I ask you something?' said Stuart.

oOo

Teddy, Sly and Stuart made their way across the road to Stuart's house. They went in quietly.

Stuart's stepdad was lying on the sofa. He had a cigarette in one paw and a half-empty glass of whisky in the other. There was a bottle of whisky on a side table nearby. The kittens watched him for a while. The stepdad was oblivious to them. They crept behind the sofa softly, but not before putting the cucumber beside the table where the bottle was.

They did not have to wait too long before the stepdad got up unsteadily to pour himself another drink.

It was then that he saw the cucumber and leapt high into the air before crashing down heavily. Alcohol affected the ability to land on all fours, observed the kittens. The cigarette and the glass of whisky went flying, but both were caught deftly by the twins. Stuart whisked the cucumber away, and all three went running from the house.

They heard Stuart's stepdad growling on the floor and hoped that he did not see them escape through the door.

oOo

Back at home, the twins went into their bedroom, while Stuart went to find PC. He thought he'd better stay away from home for a while, but that was the best fun he'd had for a long time.

'Best prank ever,' said Sly.

'Best prank ever,' agreed Teddy. 'Scooter should have filmed it for *The Scooter Show.*'

'What do you think you two are doing?' demanded Mummy Cat, sternly. They had not noticed her enter their room. She was holding a basket of washed and ironed clothes. Teddy was holding the glass of whisky, and Sly held the lit cigarette. He quickly put it behind his back, but a tell-tale slither of smoke rose above them.

'Give me those.' Mummy Cat grabbed the glass and the cigarette from the twins. 'Both of you are grounded. Stay in your room. You naughty, naughty kittens.'

oOo

Everyone was satisfied with the edit of *The Scooter Show*. The whole programme was twenty minutes long, just as Scooter wanted it to be. Scooter thought his monologue could be sharper. He would have to pay attention to the news more closely, but he was satisfied with how he sounded. Not too fast, not too slow. He uploaded the final version to YouTube.

Scooter reported to his family. 'There were lots of pauses and repetition. I recorded the whole dance routine, PC, but after a minute or so, it was enough. The tutorial was good. I showed a bit of the dance, then the tutorial and finally the whole dance again. It works well that way. Same with the cooking. I showed the finished dish first because I got the shot of Sly taking the cake out of the oven. Then I showed the cooking lesson afterwards, and I cut out all the chopping and mixing and waiting around. I got the idea because Sly said, "And this is one I made earlier" when he took it out of the oven.'

'Nice touch,' conceded Sly.

'But despite that, there's been only nine views. That's all of us and one other. Who could that be?' wondered Scooter.

o0o

Was that the door?' asked Mummy Cat, swivelling her ear towards the sound.

'Who could that be?' asked Teabag.

'Life is becoming a great mystery for us,' said Teddy, thinking it might be the post. Or the Panthers.

Mummy Cat went to have a look since no one else was bothering to get up.

It was Stuart's mother. No one had ever spoken to her, except to nod good morning, or good evening, when they saw her from time to time, coming and going.

Her eyes were ringed red. You could see she had been crying. She was still relatively young, but the ravages of a hard life had taken its toll. Mummy Cat ushered her into the kitchen where Teddy handed her a cup of tea.

Without preamble, she said, 'I've seen the video. I had no idea Stuart and all the others were suffering. Why didn't Stuart say something to me?'

'To protect you. To not make a bad situation worse. You will have to talk to Stuart,' offered Grandad sagely.

'I tried to talk to Stuart just now, but he won't say anything. I saw bruises on the kittens the other day. I thought it was through fighting. You know how kittens are?'

'Indeed,' said Scooter and Grandad at the same time.

Sly smirked.

'You all have such a loving relationship, a happy family here. I have watched you,' said Stuart's mother tearfully.

'Because we talk and communicate,' said Teabag.

'Perhaps Stuart isn't quite telling me the truth,' said his mother, sad to think that she might not have a close relationship with her kittens after all.

'In my experience, kittens seldom lie. They are more likely to stay silent than tell fibs,' said Grandad.

'But why?' asked Stuart's mother forlornly.

'Because they think cats won't believe them. Or they are threatened by the abuser. Or they might feel, mistakenly, I might add, that they deserve the abuse,' offered Grandad. 'All sorts of reasons.'

'But that's preposterous. Tom said he wouldn't hit the kittens.' said Stuart's mother, not wanting to believe that her children were being abused right under her nose.

'And you believe him over your kittens. Even with the evidence? Bruises? A torn ear? Unhappiness? Fighting?' reasoned Grandad.

'Moggie, isn't it?' asked Mummy Cat kindly.

'Yes,' said Moggie. 'Moggie Havana-Brown.'

'I'm Missy, but they all call me Mummy Cat. Moggie, your first responsibility is to protect your kittens. Every kitten has a right to health, education, family life, play, an adequate standard of living, and to be protected from abuse and harm. Shame on you if you don't try your best.' Mummy Cat tried not to sound angry, although she was.

Moggie began to cry again. 'I wish there had been a handbook for kittens when I was growing up. It would save me making stupid mistakes.'

'To make mistakes is feline. What are you going to do about it is the question,' said Grandad softly.

'I will have to do the right thing and tell him to leave. But I'm afraid. He has a temper.'

'And who does he unleash his temper on?' asked Grandad.

'Me and the kittens. Tom gets angry if his dinner is late, and if I don't iron his shirt. He hates it if the kittens make too much noise, and if he runs out of whisky. He had a nasty fall the other day. He said he saw a snake. Now he is a nightmare to live with.'

Teddy and Sly looked at each other.

'You see, my dear, his behaviour is not conducive to equitable family life. For the sake of your family, you have to be strong,' said Mummy Cat. 'We are here for you.'

'What if he won't leave?' sobbed Moggie, trembling.

'He won't be able to do much if we all go over and help him to pack,' said Sly, extending his claws.

'You know, that is not such a bad idea,' said Grandad. 'Bullies are big cowards.'

oOo

For the first time, Moggie smiled. And she was stunning.

CHAPTER TWELVE

The Eviction

'Come on let's go,' said Grandad, resolutely. 'There's no time like the present.'

'You stay here with me,' said Mummy Cat to Moggie, who was getting up to join Grandad and the kittens.

'Shouldn't I go with them?'

'No. Grandad can handle it,' said Mummy Cat, placing another cup of tea in front of Moggie and a pastry Sly had baked that morning. Mummy Cat put a paw on Moggie's shoulder to stop her from running out, and it calmed her. 'What work do you do?'

'I am a cleaner. I mean, I have a cleaning business, but I also do my fair share of cleaning, and I spend a lot of time training my team too. We don't have a name yet, but I am thinking of *Cats Clean Casas*. Or *Cleaning Cats*. Or *Cats Cleaning Company,*' rattled off Moggie, sitting down again, and sipping her tea.

'What about *Moggie's Mops?*' offered Mummy Cat.

'Oh, that is brilliant. I love it,' enthused Moggie, clapping her paws. 'That is exactly the right name. Thank you.' Then she said, 'You know I am not a victim, and neither is Stuart. We are strong. We are powerful. We are brave.'

'Of course, you are,' said Mummy Cat, smiling.

'It is Stuart who gives me strength. He is such a great kitten. He has never given me any trouble. Delicious pastry. Moggie's Mops. Love it!'

oOo

Grandad, Scooter, Shaky, PC, Teabag and the twins made their way across the road to the Havana-Browns' house. Grandad knocked on the door loudly.

Stuart opened the door tentatively. The door widened when he saw who it was. Stuart was sporting a cut lip. There was some dried blood in the corner of his mouth and on his fur.

'Is your stepdad in?' asked Grandad.

'He's in the kitchen,' replied Stuart, pointing down the hall. 'He's in a foul mood, again.'

'Let me handle it,' said Grandad and turning to the kittens, said, 'Help Stuart pack Tom's things, please. He's leaving.'

Stuart's smile radiated from his eyes. He dared not move his mouth as it still hurt. 'Come on,' he said to the kittens, 'this way.' Stuart led them upstairs and there they quickly packed clothes into a carrier bag.

Meanwhile, Grandad went into the kitchen. 'Tom?'

Tom was drinking beer and munching on a burger. He burped, looking at Grandad.

Grandad arched his back and extended his claws. Hissing loudly, he told Tom in no uncertain terms to go. 'Get lost and never come back here again, or you will have me to deal with and the authorities for abusing kittens.'

Tom started to protest, but Grandad was a formidable sight, even with his ruffled hair and round glasses. He had never stopped playing, jumping and running. He was long, muscular and sleek. Tom had grown soft and round and weak. He could see he would be no match for Grandad and he was pretty sure Stuart would join in if there were to be a fight. And hadn't Tom heard Scooter's voice in the hall? Grandad had no intention of fighting Tom, but he was not to know that.

Tom ran out of the house, tripping over the bag containing his clothes. Two pairs of trousers and four shirts. Teddy had put his toothbrush into a wash bag she found in the bathroom.

'Those are your things,' said Teddy, not unkindly. She was happy that Grandad did not get into a fight.

Sly, however, tossed a cucumber into the air towards Tom. The kittens, Stuart and Grandad watched him hop-scotch and zigzag down the road, believing that another snake was pursuing him while clutching firmly onto his few belongings.

oOo

The morning of the first day back at school, Scooter came running into the kitchen. All his siblings were eating breakfast.

'Guess what?'

'*The Scooter Show* has gone viral,' said Sly.

'How did you know?' asked Scooter, a bit deflated. It was his news to tell.

'We check on it too, you know. We're part of the show,' said Teddy.

'And you have got loads of emails, Teabag. People have some serious problems,' said Scooter.

'Really?' asked Teabag, surprised.

'Which slot is the most popular?' asked Sly.

'It is hard to say at the moment. Maybe I could ask subscribers for feedback, I don't know,' said Scooter thoughtfully.

'What if people say they don't like something, would you drop it?' asked PC.

'Not liking something is no reason to drop it. Feedback should be constructive. To help us improve. In any case, no slot is too long. If viewers don't like a topic, they can fast forward, or go and make a cup of tea. I don't know. Every slot is great. I have to thank you all for your hard work.'

'What if kittens liked everything except you, Scooter? Would you leave the show?' asked Sly, labouring the point.

'If we've gone viral, that means that they like most things,' said Scooter, not taking the bait. 'I think kittens have their favourites, and why not? That's not a bad thing, and the challenge is to keep up the standard. I believe that cats watch the show too, not just kittens. *The Scooter Show* appeals to grown-ups too. We've got school again, so we will have to work harder to get the show out on time. And I am going to put out an appeal for Milo. We have got to find him. We need a plan.'

Every one of the kittens nodded in agreement.

'But what?' sighed Teddy.

CHAPTER THIRTEEN

Sabotage

Shaky designed the logo for Moggie, and she was able to buy a small van and had the logo printed on the sides in bold letters, with a mop on the top for good measure.

Moggie got some leaflets printed and dropped them into the homes around the area, and Scooter helped with creating a website with all the prices listed, and a request form.

'I have four staff at the moment and forty clients. We charge by the hour. I am going to need more clients because my team need more work,' said Moggie. 'I hope to grow my business enough by the end of the year to have eighteen in my team, with three crews of six and three vans.'

'You want to build an empire,' said Mummy Cat. 'Is there anything we can do?'

'You have helped me loads already,' said Moggie. 'You have come up with a great name, Scooter's done the website, and Shaky has designed an attractive logo. Everyone is noticing Moggie's Mops. I love it. Building an empire, as you call it, is how I will be able to provide for my kittens and hire cats to work with me.'

oOo

A request came through to give a local camera factory a deep clean. More work like this would mean that Moggie could get some new equipment and pay herself a decent wage too, for the first time. She asked all her team to come along, and she would pay them well to do an excellent job so that they could maybe get a permanent contract from the factory. Moggie had only ever worked for private houses. Cleaning offices and factories was a new thing and very lucrative.

'I can send you to a better school, and we can go on a nice holiday for once,' said Moggie, daydreaming of a better life for her and her kittens.

'I like my school,' said Stuart. 'I don't want to change.'

oOo

On the day of the big clean, the Moggie's Mops crew turned up bright and early, dressed in their new green uniform, with 'Moggie's Mops' emblazoned on the front bib and a mop embroidered next to the words. Even their caps had the logo and embroidery on it, in gold.

'Don't you look smart, young queens and toms,' beamed Moggie. 'Ready for work?'

All were proud to work for Moggie's Mops. Moggie was a good boss.

'I hope we can all squeeze into the van, with all the mops and buckets. All the cleaning liquids are in a box at the back. And please, for goodness' sake, wear rubber mittens at all times. Those fluids can be toxic.'

'We will be careful, Moggie,' said Fluffy, a new worker.

Moggie smiled. But when she turned up with her crew to the address, there was no factory. It was a building site. Moggie rechecked the postcode. 'This is the place. It's not here.'

It was a scam.

When Moggie got home, Mummy Cat came outside to greet her.

'Well? How did it go?'

'It didn't.' Moggie went into her house and slammed the door.

o0o

It was later that Stuart told everyone what had happened. Furthermore, there were ten more

125

jobs that came through. All of them to clean huge houses, an office block and the Manor House.

Someone is deliberately sabotaging your business, Moggie,' said Mummy Cat. 'Do you have any enemies?'

'I don't think so.'

'Well, you do,' said Mummy Cat. 'Evidently.'

'Indeed,' said Grandad.

'Tom,' said Stuart. 'I bet it was him.'

'We could never prove it,' said Moggie, alarmed that Tom would do such a thing.

'The only thing that you can do is to check out the addresses first and see the owners as well before you go to clean,' said Stuart.

'I don't think the Manor House would want Moggie's Mops to do the cleaning. So we don't even have to bother with looking into that. I had to pay my team with money I did not bring in. If this happens again, I will be bankrupt by the end of the month. So much for building an empire,' said Moggie sadly.

'Mum put her heart and soul into the business,' said Stuart angrily. 'She was so happy. And now, she is so sad. Even thinking of giving up. Someone must've gone on to her website and put in fake orders.'

'I am sorry, Fluffy,' Moggie said. 'I will have to let you go. I cannot afford to keep you on because we don't have the work and I have paid out wages for nothing.'

Fluffy burst into tears, and without saying a word, handed back her uniform that she was so proud of, and the new mop that she hadn't even had a chance to use.

All Moggie's other team members carried on with the original contracts, but their motivation was gone, and they missed young Fluffy. She was funny and cute.

A few small jobs came in, and Stuart did as much as he could at home, helping his brothers and sisters to learn to read and doing household chores. Both he and his mother were exhausted most of the time and started arguing with each other over silly little things. Stuart began to think that he was becoming more and more like his stepdad each day, and what a terrifying thought that was.

oOo

Over breakfast, Stuart said, 'I have already done my homework for the weekend. Why don't I come with you to help with your cleaning round?'

'Oh, would you? Most of the team don't work weekends, and I have a few new jobs to see to,' said Moggie gratefully.

'Yes,' said Stuart. He'd resolved to do something his stepdad would never do, every day, and one of the things was to help his mother.

'What about the dancing with PC you've planned?'

'I'll let her know. I am sure she will understand.'

'Thank you, Stuart. You are such a good kitten,' said Moggie, grateful, but still not wanting to spoil his fun.

Stuart went to tell PC that he had to help his mother. PC was not happy that she could not practise a dance routine in the run-up to filming the latest Scooter Show.

'I have an idea,' she said. 'See you in a minute.'

Stuart went back home, not sure what she meant, but he had no time to ask for an explanation.

'Ready, Mum?' Stuart shouted up the stairs.

'Yes, let's go,' said Moggie, ruffling Stuart's hair. 'We have to take the kittens to the minders. They are expecting us.'

When Stuart opened the door, there was Scooter, Teabag, Sly, Teddy and PC outside, dressed in old clothes and overalls. Running to catch up was Shaky in one of his painting aprons. Scooter was carrying his video camera. 'I think it might be worth filming all of us at work. It could be interesting for *The Scooter Show.*'

'We are joining Moggie's Mops for the day,' said PC saluting with one paw.

'I don't believe this. Thank you so much,' said Moggie tearfully. Moggie always seemed to be crying or on the brink of tears. Tears of sadness or tears of happiness. Right now, she was happy. Her tears still confused Stuart.

'Don't cry, Mum,' pleaded Stuart. 'That's what's friends are for.'

'Come on then,' said Moggie. 'Or we will be late. Lots to do.'

o0o

With all the kittens working hard, they finished up in no time.

I am going to take you all for a meal,' announced Moggie. 'You deserve it. And milkshakes all round.'

'Yippee,' said Teddy.

'I make the best milkshakes,' said Sly.

'Nice to go out though,' said Teddy.

CHAPTER FOURTEEN

The Manor House

Driving back home, Moggie passed the Manor House, standing majestically on the hill.

'If we had that job, all our financial worries would be over,' said Moggie, pointing it out to the kittens.

'Why don't you go up and ask them who made the booking online and why they don't want the job done after all?'

'The other places didn't even exist,' said Moggie.

'Well, this one does,' said Stuart.

'All right then, I will do just that,' said Moggie resolutely, sitting up tall in the driver's seat.

She swung the van around and drove up the long tree-lined drive to a large oak door. All the kittens tumbled out of the vehicle. Scooter hammered on the door, and moments later, a butler opened it. He was an elderly cat, with whiskers long and white; his coat was flecked with grey, peeking out from his formal butler's uniform.

'Hello,' said Scooter. 'We are Moggie's Mops, and we want to know why you requested our services and then no longer wanted them?'

'We expected you yesterday,' said the butler, with a slight frown.

'What? I don't understand,' said Moggie.

'I booked you for yesterday and you did not show up. We have an event tonight, and I have to say, Ma'am is very disappointed.'

'I can explain,' said Stuart.

'It is too late; your services are no longer required. Good day,' said the butler attempting to close the door.

Scooter put his paw out to keep the door open.

'Who is that?' came a voice from inside the great house.

'The cleaners, Ma'am. I told them to go away,' said the butler.

'Have you found a replacement, Charles?' came the voice from within the house again.

'Not yet, Ma'am',

'Then let them clean.'

'As you wish, Ma'am.'

Turning to Moggie, Charles said to her, holding up two claws, 'You have two hours.'

In a flurry, the kittens got to work. The Manor House was soon spotless.

'I must say, you have done a good job,' said Charles the butler, smiling for the first time.

He had followed them around the great house and halls inspecting their work.

Moggie explained the misunderstanding and Charles agreed to give Moggie's Mops a try. 'Every morning, early. The Manor House is enormous. There are rooms you have not seen that will need cleaning too. Ma'am entertains a lot.'

'We planned a big party tonight, Moggie,' said Ma'am, 'but we are going to have to cancel after all. One hundred guests. A pity. I was looking forward to it.'

'Why?' asked Moggie.

'The caterers cancelled. The entertainment has cancelled. The DJ cancelled. My gown has not arrived. It is a disaster,' said Ma'am, looking at Moggie and the kittens.

All the kittens looked at each other. It was the weekend, after all.

'I have a suggestion,' said Scooter. 'You won't have to cancel your party. My brother Sly is a chef. My sister PC can perform a wonderful dance routine for your guests. Teddy can make any dress you have in your closet fit you better than ever, and I can download some music, whatever you like. Shaky will be able to draw caricatures of your guests for fun. They would love that. Teabag, Moggie and Stuart can help Charles with the guests, and I will film the whole event and interview some of them for *The Scooter Show.*

Ma'am was silent for a long while, mulling over what she had heard. She was long and slender, with slanted grey eyes, regal, and very much the queen of the Manor House. She at last looked at Charles, who nodded.

'Well,' said Charles. 'Let's get to work. Lots to be done.'

'I have not heard of *The Scooter Show*, but I have some friends who would love to be part of a reality show, I am sure. Come,' said Ma'am to Teddy. 'Help me decide on an outfit for the party.'

o0o

The party was a great success. Moggie and the kittens were beyond tired, but it was fun. They drove home in silence.

The kittens tumbled into bed, exhausted. They would catch up with Stuart and Moggie the next day.

Scooter had filmed the party and would be editing ferociously in the morning. He had the cooking and the dancing, and there were some interesting cats at the event. Scooter did interviews asking about their clothing style, what they did for a living, and how they came to know Ma'am. All of Ma'am's friends were good- looking, rich and talented. The next *The Scooter Show* would be excellent.

PC had excelled herself with a dance routine. 'Bravo,' called everyone. Sly made delicious canapés. Shaky did quick cartoon sketches that amused everyone, and he got a commission to do some portraits. A lot of the guests asked Moggie for her business card. She would be getting some new clients.

Ma'am looked stunning in a red outfit that Teddy was able to customise quickly for her, and she asked Teddy to come back to help her recycle more clothes. 'I am rich, but I am not an idiot,' she had told Teddy. 'No point in buying expensive clothes, just to wear them once. We all have to do our bit to save the planet.'

o0o

'I am so happy', said Teddy, on top of her bunk bed. 'I've never worked so hard. Who knew that doing a favour for someone would bring so many rewards.'

Sly was snoring.

o0o

Two things happened at Ma'am's party that are worth mentioning. The first thing was that the kittens had an opportunity to look around the Manor House as they were cleaning it. They entered the library, and there, over the fireplace, was *The Chimeras* painting.

'That's my painting,' said Shaky excitedly, bouncing up and down. 'I am glad it went to a good home.'

The second thing was when Stuart brought down a stack of plates to the kitchen. He heard the clatter of pots and pans being scrubbed behind a wall of shelves.

Then Stuart heard a burp.

'No,' he thought, 'it couldn't be!'

He tiptoed along the shelves, and to his surprise, he saw Tom, paws deep in soapy water, washing up.

'Tom?'

'Hello, Stuart,' said Tom, genuinely pleased to see him.

'What are you doing here?' asked Stuart in disbelief.

'It looks obvious to me,' he said, looking down at the pots, a little embarrassed. 'You would think they'd have a dishwasher.'

'Yes, you're the dishwasher. No, there is one. It's just that it takes too long. There are a lot of guests,' offered Stuart.

'What are you doing here?' asked Tom, pointing with his chin to what Stuart had in his paws. 'You can't be a guest if they have you carrying plates.'

'I'm helping out some friends.' Stuart didn't want to mention his mum.

'It's okay. I have already seen Moggie. I have apologised for my behaviour, and she's forgiven me. I hope you can forgive me too.'

Stuart shrugged. 'Only if you stop drinking and get a decent job. You are supposed to be a professional.'

With that, Stuart turned to go back to the party.

o0o

Tom wiped his mouth with a paw. He lifted his drink towards his lips, paused, and then tipped the whole lot down the sink.

Stuart watched him from the door and smiled.

CHAPTER FIFTEEN

The Arrest

One evening, while the kittens were finishing dinner, there was a pounding on the door.

Shaky rushed to open it. He thought it was the Panthers again, demanding more pictures for Felix. He was surprised to see a burly police cat standing in front of him. The flashing police car light lit up Shaky's face every time it whirled around. He could see another police cat in the driver's seat.

'Are you Shaky the artist?' asked the police cat.

'Yes,' said Shaky meekly.

'We have a warrant for your arrest.'

'Why?' shrieked Shaky. 'What have I done?'

By then all the kittens, Grandad and Mummy Cat were gathered by the front door.

'What is he supposed to have done, officer?' demanded Mummy Cat.

The police cat grabbed Shaky, who wriggled to get free and was wailing uncontrollably.

'Mum, Mum, I didn't do anything wrong.'

'Shaky, I'm arresting you on suspicion of forgery. You do not have to say anything, but it may harm your defence if you do not mention when questioned something which you later rely on in court. Do you understand?'

'Yes. No. I have not done anything,' repeated Shaky, getting hysterical. 'Mum, Mum, help me.'

Holding Shaky still, the police cat said, 'We have to take him to the station.'

'I am coming too,' said Mummy Cat, grabbing her coat and a bag from the hall table.

'As you wish,' said the police cat.

'Dad, please get help for us,' said Mummy Cat to her father.

Grandad had been stunned by the whole episode, but he quickly got into action on the phone. He called a lawyer friend of his; a dour old feral cat turned lawyer.

Soon after Shaky and Mummy Cat arrived at the police station, another police cat put them into a small room. There was an old-style tape machine on a large table in the middle of the room and a big mirror on one wall. Shaky suspected that it could be a two-way mirror. He and Mummy Cat were seated facing it.

It was almost an hour before a female feline came in with some water. It was another thirty minutes before two officers came in with the lawyer that Grandad had contacted. 'Hello, young kitten. I'm Leon, the lawyer. I am a friend of your grandad. I will do my best to get you home.' Turning to the officers, Leon, the lawyer asked them, 'What are the charges?'

The female feline pressed a button on the tape machine and looking at a big clock above the door said 'The time is 10 o'clock. I am Inspector Spot. My colleagues are Inspector Lucky and Inspector Patches. Also present is Leon, the lawyer who will be representing Shaky.'

'What are the charges?' repeated Leon, the lawyer.

'Shaky is accused of forging masterpieces and selling them off as original paintings for the notorious art dealer Felix. Felix is missing. Do you know his whereabouts, Shaky?'

'No,' said Shaky, emphatically. 'I have never even met Felix.'

Leon, the lawyer told Shaky not to say another word. Turning to the inspectors, he asked, 'Have you got any proof? If Felix is missing, you don't have any more details, do you? I will have to ask you to let my client go home to his family.'

Shaky was allowed home, but they told him that he would have to attend court and that he should plead guilty and not waste everyone's time. Shaky's court case was imminent, and if he were found guilty, he would go to prison for a very long time. That would be the end of his ambitions, his hopes and his dreams.

Leon, the lawyer told Shaky that he should get a good night's sleep and that he would see him in the morning.

'It doesn't look good for you, Shaky. I have to admit,' said Leon, the lawyer.

Shaky hung his head, tears welling in his eyes and spilling down his cheeks, and dripping from his whiskers.

Mummy Cat hugged him close.

Sitting nearby were Scooter, Teddy, Sly, PC and Teabag. Grandad was in his den looking over law books to find out about Shaky's rights.

oOo

'Felix asked you to copy some masterpieces that he had buyers for, and he gave you lots of money, in cash? It doesn't look good, Shaky.'

'I never forged those paintings deliberately,' wailed Shaky.

'Intentions and actions. It's the same thing,' said Leon, the lawyer, shaking his head. 'I will try and get you the best deal if you plead guilty.'

'I am not guilty. I had no idea.'

'The jury will see you as stupid or very smart. Either way, it is not looking good. They will believe your family were behind this too. After all, Grandad gave up his den. Sly cooked you a nice lunch, and everyone was to benefit. Dance classes for PC. Medical school fees paid for Teabag. Laptops all round at Christmas. Even for Milo, the chihuahua. It's not looking good, Shaky.'

'You're supposed to be on our side,' retorted Teddy.

'Shaky, you won't tell us anything about the details,' said Leon, the lawyer.

'We have no details,' echoed the kittens.

'The Panthers never told us anything, I told you,' said Shaky.

oOo

The day of the court case had arrived.

'It is always a good idea to plead not guilty, Shaky, for the arraignment,' said Grandad, who had found out some useful tips in his law books.

'Why are they giving Shaky a raincoat?' asked Teddy.

'An arraignment.' Grandad laughed, in spite of his anxiety for Shaky. 'Not a raincoat. It is when the judge reads out the charges, and you plead not guilty, Shaky, because you're not. That will give us time to review the facts and the evidence and begin working to discredit the charges against you. If you plead guilty, you're admitting to the crime.'

Shaky wore one of Grandad's suits that Teddy had altered for him. It was still too big. The court usher led Shaky to the witness box, and the judge read out the charges and then asked Shaky if he was guilty or not guilty.

'Not guilty,' said Shaky. His voice rang out, sounding more confident than he felt.

o0o

Leon, the lawyer was in the kitchen going over the evidence again and again with Shaky. 'You did well today, Shaky. I think if you repeat what you said to me, the jury will believe that you were not deliberately trying to fake the picture. You are a talented artist, and Felix commissioned you to do some work. They should be lenient with you, and as you are a minor, you should get a reduced sentence.'

'The jury is going to think I am guilty and send me to prison?' said Shaky in disbelief. 'Is there no way out for me? All I did was paint some pictures.'

'These are such wonderful pictures, Shaky,' said PC, flicking through a thick album.

'Those are the pictures of the paintings?' asked Leon, the lawyer.

'Yes. I always take a photo of Shaky's work to keep because we never see them again, although we know who bought *The Chimeras.'*

'Can I see?' asked Leon, the lawyer holding out his paw.

Leon, the lawyer flicked through the pages of the album. 'These are marvellous, Shaky. You are indeed very talented. I will do my best to get all the charges dropped.' Leon, the lawyer smiled widely, showing his fangs. It was better that he didn't smile.

o0o

Leon, the lawyer stood before the judge and told the court that Shaky was innocent and they should drop the charges immediately.

The kittens wondered what made Leon, the lawyer start to believe that Shaky was innocent so emphatically. 'What made him suddenly change his tune?' thought Scooter, who was sitting with his family at the back of the court.

The prosecutor reported that the evidence was compelling.

'I have some new evidence,' said Leon, the lawyer.

'Go ahead,' said the judge incredulously. 'Let's hear it.'

Leon, the lawyer walked up to the front of the courtroom and facing the jury of twelve cats, looked at each one of them for a moment or two, prolonging the drama of what he was about to do. In his hand was PC's photo album. 'I have here an album that Shaky's sister showed me. She takes pictures of all of Shaky's work.' Leon, the lawyer passed the album among the jury. There were murmurs of appreciation and smiles. This took a long time because there were a lot of photos, and each jury member was enjoying what they saw.

'What is going on?' thought Shaky.

Finally, Leon, the lawyer turned to the room and addressing no one in particular, stated, 'If my client wanted to deceive anyone, he would not have painted the *Girl with a Pearl Earring* with a diamond earring, or *The Scream* smiling, or even the *Mona Lisa* with an afro and a Black Lives Matter t-shirt. Need I go on? Van Gogh's sunflowers are yellow roses, and the Warhol Campbell soup picture is row upon row of pot noodles, chicken and mushroom flavour. Felix had buyers for Shaky's work because Shaky is a great artist.'

The courtroom erupted in laughter and applause.

The judge pounded his gavel on a sounding block. 'Order! Order!'

No one paid any attention. Sly put his paw to his lips and blew a loud whistle. The jury continued clapping and some started to whistle too.

'Order! Order!' boomed the judge.

The press was waiting outside to greet Shaky who was hoisted onto Grandad's shoulders.

Everyone was jubilant.

o0o

'How did they come to arrest me in the first place?' asked Shaky, when they were back at home. Sly served chocolate milkshakes all round, while Mummy Cat, Grandad and Leon, the lawyer had a little catnip in theirs.

Leon, the lawyer told them: 'It seems that some undercover police cats overheard the Panthers talking about your collection, in a pub. The police put two and two together and came up with seven. They believed that if they

145

could solve this so-called crime of the century, they would be in line for a promotion. Never mind the facts. If they saw the paintings, they would have known at once that it wasn't a con, and the Panthers couldn't recognise a Starbucks logo from the little mermaid if you paid them. Cheers.'

CHAPTER SIXTEEN

Panic Attack!

'Did you know Teabag is meowing in her room,' said Teddy. 'I heard her.'

Grandad and all the kittens rushed to her bedroom door. They could hear great racking sobs and meows.

Grandad calmly opened the door and put his paws on Teabag's shoulders. He remained calm, breathing in deeply and then exhaling. Moments later, Teabag stopped crying and found herself copying the rhythms of Grandad's breath.

'That's good,' said Grandad. 'Breathe in for seven, hold for four and breathe out for seven. Panic attacks can cause us to have trouble breathing, and breathing is life itself. Now, kitty cat, what is going on for you that is making you not catch your breath?'

'I don't know,' sobbed Teabag. 'I'm finding everything so overwhelming. I have been doing mind maps, like you said. That's working, I think, but I can't sleep. My mind is working overtime.'

'And, I might add,' said Grandad. 'You, kitty cat, are one big fluff of fur and bones. You're not eating either, are you?'

Sly, Teddy, and Scooter were listening at the door. To hear what was going on inside Teabag's room, Sly leaned on Teddy and Teddy leaned on Scooter, and then they all tumbled into the room.

'What's the matter, Teabag?' asked Teddy, under a mound of kittens.

'Nothing,' said Teabag, alarmed and embarrassed.

'You know, the hardest thing, even harder than what you are going through, is to ask for help from the cats and kittens that care for you.' Grandad left the room, leaving Teabag surrounded by all her siblings.

oOo

Teabag promised to eat something if Sly cooked her favourite meal.

Mummy Cat looked on, concerned, but was pleased that Teabag was eating again.

Teabag smiled at everyone. 'I'm okay. I am. It's just that I am in my room studying because I have a goal, but I don't want to be stuck in my room all my life studying. There is more to me than that, but I don't know what it is.'

'I think I know what you mean,' said Shaky. Everyone looked at him. 'See! If I say something, you all stare at me. I can feel it. If I do something different, out of the ordinary, everyone is so surprised, and that makes me self-conscious. I used to have self-doubt, but not anymore.'

'That is the longest speech you have ever made, Shaky,' observed Sly.

'I don't feel like I have to please anyone but myself,' said Shaky petulantly.

'My dears,' said Grandad, holding up his paw to stop a possible row. 'I had a chuckle now and then, but growing up, I was so serious. I was so driven. No time off. No fun. I had to get all my exams and go to university. If I took a break, I felt that the world would end and come crashing down on me. I pushed myself more than my parents or teachers ever did. I eventually learned about balance. It made me a more interesting cat.'

'Panic attacks can't be healthy,' said Teddy.

'No,' agreed Grandad. 'But if you do not heed what your body is telling you, it will shout. A panic attack is your body shouting. And I think your body is telling you loud and clear, Teabag; enough is enough. You *will* go to university. You *will* do all the things you set out to do, but you can be a whole kitty cat and not one-dimensional. Have fun. Learn different things.'

'You need a chill pill,' said Sly. 'That's what Grandad means.'

'I have a plan,' said Scooter.

'What is it?' asked Teabag, not sure she was going to like it, but she trusted Scooter and admired him too, especially because of *The Scooter Show*.

'This is my plan. PC is going to teach you to dance, Teabag. Shaky will teach you to draw. Sly will teach you to cook, and Teddy will help you to customise some of your clothes. After all, you want to look good when you go off to university. Dancing is a great social skill, and everyone has to eat.'

'Bravo,' said Grandad. 'That's probably the best chill pill ever. What do you think, Teabag? Do you think you can let your siblings help you to be more, more you, if you like?'

Teabag nodded. Her shoulders relaxed, and reaching for another piece of the pie Sly had made she smiled gratefully at everyone. 'I think that would be fun. Thank you.'

'I'll teach you to dance too, Shaky. After all, Teabag is going to need a partner.'

'I have four left paws,' said Shaky, laughing.

'Everyone can dance,' acknowledged PC. 'Everyone.'

'Can I chip in here?' asked Mummy Cat. 'I am going to teach everyone how to tidy up, wash and iron clothes and do the shopping. Won't that be fun?'

This time all the kittens moaned in unison, 'NO!'

oOo

Scooter had almost finished filming another edition of *The Scooter Show*. He had asked Teabag to read out an appeal for Milo.

'I also want to discuss a special problem as well, Scooter,' she said.

'Go for it, Teabag,' said Scooter. He started filming and waited for Teabag to begin.

'Dear listeners, this is Teabag's Advice Corner. I am not going to read a letter from one of you this time. I want to talk about a problem in my household. Well, more than one problem, actually.

'The first problem is that we have carelessly lost our dear friend. He has gone missing, and we can't find him. He is a chihuahua, and his name is Milo. If anyone knows where he is, we just want to see that he is alright and to tell him that he has friends who love him. We never realised that he was homeless because he hid it so well and quite frankly, we never asked about his family or his situation. If anyone has any news about him, please, please, get in touch.'

Teabag paused because Scooter would be putting a phone number and email address up for kittens to call in or to write in.

'The next problem is mine,' continued Teabag. 'My family started to notice something was wrong with me, even though I have been pretending that everything was normal. They consider me to be the clever one. The one destined to be whatever I wanted to be, and I never wanted to let anyone down. That's a heavy burden to carry. To live up to others' expectations. And the expectations I have for myself. I want to do well, but I am afraid, too.

'I have not been sleeping, nor eating properly, meowing for no reason and having panic attacks. Yet I have my Grandad that I can talk to, but I didn't. Mummy Cat to talk to, but I didn't. I also have my siblings that care for me. Thankfully, my family came up with a solution. My medication is a chill pill, as Sly puts it. I am going to learn some new skills. I need to do different things once in a while. Shaky is teaching me to paint, and Sly is going to teach me to cook. I don't even know how to boil an egg. Imagine! I want to be a doctor, and I can't even feed myself. Teddy will help me to create some new outfits by recycling my wardrobe. What I am looking forward to as well, is PC teaching me to dance. I think my family have got a lot of brilliant adult life skills. Scooter has allowed me to focus on others, rather than myself and to realise how lucky I am. And Grandad is teaching me to relax and study more effectively. Milo, if we can find him, could help me brush up on my Spanish because when I qualify, I want to travel around Central America and work with sick animals while I am there.

'My advice to anyone going through what I am going through is to talk to someone. And if you have a friend who you suspect is having a hard time, listen to them. Listen to what they are saying but also to what they are not saying. Milo wanted to keep his Christmas present at our house and not take it home. Why not? We didn't ask. By talking to my family, I found that the thing that was worrying me the most was leaving them and going off to medical school. I am scared. But it is okay to be scared.'

'And cut,' said Scooter.

'That appeal for Milo has taken on a whole new angle. Thanks, Teabag. I know that you are going to be a great doctor. What is it they say? *Physician, heal thyself.*'

'Precisely,' said Teabag, sagely. 'I'm scared of my own shadow nowadays, but that's not the point. The point is to feel the fear and do it anyway.'

'You know,' said Scooter, 'I have an idea for finding Milo.'

CHAPTER SEVENTEEN

The Search Party

'We will go to the entrance Milo took us to, and we have to ensure he can't escape through any gaps or other gates,' said Scooter. 'Maggie Magpie can't help us.'

'Why not?' asked Sly.

'She tried, but she says that they can't see through the trees and bushes. They are too thick. And Milo's tent is dark green and he probably only moves around at night,' answered Scooter.

'So our best bet is your plan, Scooter,' said Teddy. 'We need dogs. That is our only hope.'

'But how will we get the message out there? How will we spread the word?' asked PC, in despair.

'Maggie Magpie. She and her friends are in the park every morning early. That's when the dogs go for their walk. If she and her mates can tell the dogs what we want to do, we will see who shows up. We should arrange the search for Milo for tomorrow night,' said Scooter decisively.

'How many dogs do we need?' asked Teabag.

'The reserve is big. There are lots of places Milo can hide. We need as many as we can get,' said Scooter.

'Milo needs to know he has friends looking out for him,' said PC.

o0o

The next morning the kittens heard the loud chirruping and cawing of excited bird song.

'Those magpies are very noisy this morning,' said Grandad, reaching for more toast. 'I wish they would pipe down. I can't concentrate on reading the papers.'

Scooter winked at his siblings. They knew that Maggie Magpie had got her friends to spread the message to the dogs in the park. That's what they were doing. But would it work?

To wait until the evening was going to be an ordeal. None of the kittens knew if any of the dogs would help them find Milo.

'What can we do?' asked Teddy, feeling more anxious than ever before.

'We wait,' said Scooter, breathing out through his mouth several times to steady his nerves.

o0o

'Let's go over your plan again.' It was Grandad.

Scooter was surprised.

'Sly told me. Don't worry. It is a good thing what you are doing, but perilous. There could be a lot of dogs involved. Some could be vicious.'

'I can't stop you, can I?' It was Mummy Cat. 'Here is a torch.'

'If we die, we all die together,' said Sly nervously.

Teddy looked at her family, knowing that this was probably the most dangerous mission for them, ever.

oOo

'It's 10 o'clock, let's go. If no dogs show up, we have to search for Milo ourselves,' said Scooter.

'Perhaps we should split up,' said PC.

'No,' said Teddy. 'I'm scared.'

When the cats got to the gate of the reserve, not one dog was there; it was dark and silent.

'Oh well. Let's go and look for him, for a bit,' said PC sadly. 'And we can try again in the morning.'

Suddenly there was a low whispered howl. And then another, and another. It was as if the trees were quivering in the darkness as twenty or more dogs and puppies emerged from the shadows. Leading the pack was Barney, a big curly white ball of fluffy fur. Barney stood in front of Scooter.

'Maggie Magpie told us to meet you here to look for Milo. We know Milo, and we will help you find him.'

'Thank you,' said Scooter, smiling broadly. 'Milo is our dear friend, and this may be our last chance to ever see him again. I can't thank you enough.'

The dogs panted excitedly, tails wagging. 'We will surround the reserve, and then the bigger dogs will go through the middle,' stated Barney matter-of-factly.

'Mind, there are ponds in the middle,' warned Scooter.

'That's okay. We will sniff the ponds out, and we can swim.'

'If anyone finds Milo bark three times,' said Scooter.

'No. A howl would be best. The sound travels further,' said Barney.

'Okay,' said Scooter, believing that Barney had watched too many wolf movies.

The kittens were waiting for what seemed like ages. It was challenging to walk on the ground all the time because of the mud and scrubs, but it was fun to leap up onto low branches and balance along the length of fallen tree trunks. But eventually, they thought it best to stay close to the entrance with the torch shining in the gloom.

The cats could see quite well, even without the torch, but it comforted them to have it shining in the darkness. The dogs could smell what was around and within minutes they picked up a scent. A low tentative howl went up.

'Did you hear that?' said Teddy.

'Over there,' shouted Scooter. The kittens scampered to where the sound was coming from. Barney came forward and shamefully admitted that he and the others had made a mistake.

'Sorry, Scooter. We have never had to do this before; hunt. We get food delivered. The only skill we have had to master in all these years is how to work an electric tin opener,' offered Barney by way of an explanation.

'Fast food is not always good for you,' admonished Sly. 'You should watch *The Scooter Show* on YouTube and learn to cook properly.'

'Oh, what do you cook?' asked Barney.

'Hey enough of this,' said Scooter. 'You can catch up on all that later. We have to focus on finding Milo.'

'You don't have anything belonging to Milo do you so that we can pick up his scent?'

'I have this.' PC took Milo's headband from around her neck. She had not taken it off since the day Milo stormed out.

'Great.' Barney called all the dogs together. 'Hey my lovely canines, dogs and puppies, have a sniff of this.'

Barney held the headband in the air and the dogs, one by one, came up to smell it. 'Now we know what we are looking for, let's go. Go, go, go.'

The dogs and over-excited puppies wagged their tails so hard; Teddy was sure they would wag them right off.

'Whose idea was it to let the puppies come?' wondered Sly.

'We should be grateful that so many showed up,' said Teddy. 'Anyway, the little ones will be able to scrabble through tiny gaps and holes because Milo is so tiny.'

oOo

There was a rustle in the bushes, which startled

the kittens. 'Who goes there?' demanded Scooter, shining the flashlight on the shrubs.

'It's me,' called out Stuart. 'I thought I would help you look.'

'*Mejor tarde que nunca,*' muttered Teabag, hoping that they would find Milo soon so that he could help her with Spanish. She had a test coming up.

'What?'

'Better late than never.'

'Sorry.'

'No. I mean it in a good way,' said Teabag.

Stuart smiled. 'It's thanks to you lot that we are much happier now, but Mum has to work harder than ever. We all help out a lot. My siblings and I watch *The Scooter Show* for tips.'

'I made a worm pie the other day. And very nice it was too. I got the recipe from *The Scooter Show*.' It was Maggie Magpie from a treetop.

'I never did a worm pie,' said Sly, perplexed.

'No, but you did make a pie, and you said you could use any filling we wanted to.'

'Oh, I see,' said Sly, pleased that his recipes had such broad appeal.

Reluctantly Scooter called a halt to the *Scooter Show* reviews. 'We have to look out for Milo. Focus, everyone, focus.'

Suddenly, out of nowhere, they heard a familiar voice.

'Are you looking for me?'

And suddenly there was howling, and excited barking and all the dogs surrounded the clearing where the kittens were. Milo walked out from a shrub.

'Milo! Thank goodness. Where have you been?' asked Scooter, poking him in the chest with a paw.

Before Milo could answer, Barney came strolling up with Milo's tent and other belongings and put it down at his feet. With a big grin, Barney said. 'We will leave you to it. We have to get the puppies home. Glad we found Milo. Take care, Milo. You have got some wonderful friends here. And if you need to talk, don't be a stranger.' With that, Barney plodded off, taking a pack of wagging tails with him.

'Quiet, calm down, be quiet. Yes, we can come out again. Yes, it was fun,' said Barney to the puppies, and waving cheerily to the kittens said, 'Look what you've started. I have to take these puppies out every week now.'

The kittens waved in unison.

'Thank you, Barney,' they cried.

'I am going to make some chewy beef bite biscuits for my next cookery slot,' said Sly decisively.

All the kittens hugged Milo tightly, in turn, and then they brought him home.

CHAPTER EIGHTEEN

Battersea

Mummy Cat insisted that Milo took a hot bath before getting into bed.

'You know you can stay here forever,' said Scooter, settling down to sleep in the spare basket, having given up his bed to Milo.

'The day I met you and Teddy was when my family disappeared. I got home, and they were gone,' said Milo sadly.

'And you don't know where they went?' asked Scooter.

'Someone said they were in Battersea and that the rehousing dog came and took them away. I think they have a new home now. I wasn't there, and they couldn't wait for me, or they would have missed the opportunity. I would have been home, but we were exploring the nature reserve,' said Milo.

'Where's Battersea?' asked Scooter.

'It's a place in the south,' said Milo. 'I've heard it's nice.'

'Let's go and find your family. We can get there on a train. Grandad can help us find the address and the directions.'

The next morning Scooter, Teddy and Grandad got on the Metropolitan line to Baker Street and then the Bakerloo line to Oxford Circus and the Victoria Line to Vauxhall. They trotted briskly to Vauxhall Bus Station and finally took the bus to Battersea Dogs and Cats Home. They found themselves in front of a huge, mostly glass building. A sign outside stated, *'Are you ready to be loved?'*

'I'm scared,' said Teddy.

'Don't be. Many homeless cats and dogs end up here before finding a new place to live. They get medical treatment and help with mental health issues as well. If your family are here, they would have been well looked after, Milo,' said Grandad reassuringly.

The four trooped up to the reception area.

'Can I help you?' asked the receptionist. She had long painted claws and extended whiskers.

Milo pushed forward. It was right that he did the talking.

'I'm looking for my family,' he said.

'Name?'

'Pedro Chihuahua is my dad. My mum and my two sisters will be with him as well.'

The receptionist looked through some notes and then she looked on her computer, punching in the name. 'I am sorry there are no Chihuahuas here.'

'Can we have a look around anyway?' asked Grandad, curious to see the inside of the magnificent building.

'Certainly. Our home is open to the public,' said the receptionist kindly. 'I will call someone to show you around. Are you thinking of staying here?'

'Maybe,' said Milo.

'No,' said Teddy quickly. 'He is staying with us.'

Milo smiled gratefully. Battersea Home for Dogs and Cats was a long way from Harrow.

A tall skinny greyhound came bounding up to Milo. 'I will show you around. Follow me.'

They walked up and down the cages looking at the dogs resting in their baskets.

'This is where Max lived before he came to us when I was growing up. Remember I was telling you,' said Grandad.

'I should have asked if they were ever here,' said Milo.

'Who?' asked Greyhound.

'The Chihuahua family. My dad, mum and sisters,' said Milo.

'Pedro Chihuahua, his wife and the two girl puppies?' asked Greyhound.

'Yes,' said Milo hopefully. His tail wagged for the first time in a long while.

'They were here. Pedro moved to a lovely house nearby. Near the park. I see them all the time,' said Greyhound. 'I can take you to them, if you like. I know where they live. You have to wait until I finish serving dinner. I'll be quick.'

'Oh, Milo. That is the best news ever,' said Teddy. 'And Greyhound. Isn't that kind of him?'

oOo

Greyhound came back to the reception area, now out of his overalls and in his street clothes. He had on a nice jacket with the number four printed on the sides (from his racing days) jeans and the same boots Milo had, but in a different colour.

'Come on, let's go.'

The Chihuahua house was indeed lovely, and as Greyhound said, near the park.

Milo hammered on the door and barked loudly.

The front door flung open, and there were Milo's mother, father and his two sisters. 'We can recognise that bark anywhere,' beamed Milo's dad, who looked exactly like him, as did his mother and his two sisters.

o0o

'We need to be getting back,' said Grandad.

'Thank you,' said Milo. Thank you for helping me find them. I will never forget you. Never.'

'Good luck, Milo,' said Scooter sadly.

After saying their goodbyes Scooter, Grandad and Teddy walked slowly back to get a bus and then all the trains to Harrow.

'It's a lovely house,' said Scooter.

'The family is great,' said Grandad.

'They never gave up on Milo, did they?' said Scooter.

'Look how they had his bedroom ready for him,' said Grandad. 'We should be happy that he is happy.'

Teddy said nothing but sobbed all the way home. Scooter hugged her but to no avail, she continued to meow. Scooter wanted to be strong for both of them. Even Grandad was sniffing and blowing into his hanky on the way home.

o0o

'Where's Milo?' said PC when Scooter, Teddy and Grandad returned home.

'He's at home with his family,' said Scooter, sniffing loudly.

'But we said he could stay here,' wailed PC.

'Yes, and the offer is still open, but he is with his sisters and parents,' said Scooter.

'Why did they move in the first place?' asked Teabag.

'They were due to move anyway, but it happened when Milo was out, and they had no way of letting him know. They were looking for him too. They kept his room ready for him all this time.'

PC ran from the room, meowing loudly. Teddy ran after her.

'I miss Milo,' PC sobbed.

'We can visit. Milo can visit,' said Teddy, coming to terms with the situation.

'It is not the same. It will never be the same.'

'He's happy now he's with his family. You should have seen him,' said Teddy, trying her best to soothe PC.

'But he lives such a long way away. We are never going to see him again.'

CHAPTER NINETEEN

Chill Pill

As soon as he could, Milo came down for the weekend. He was keen to see his friends again. Stuart was over from his house too.

Milo had started a new school and was doing well. Although he was still tiny, he seemed more grown-up.

'Are you happy?' asked PC.

'Yes. But I missed you, of course, and I miss my old school. You won't get rid of me so easily; I will be here as often as before. And you can come over to see me too.'

All the kittens were happy to have their old friend back.

'Did you know I was following you that night?' asked Scooter.

'Of course. We dogs have a powerful sense of smell. I was very upset about PC having a new partner. Sorry, Stuart. It wasn't your fault. That and not having my family just made me feel so angry.'

Stuart had remained silent during this exchange. He thought he was intruding and should leave when Scooter asked him a question.

'You said your family is a lot happier now. What changes have you seen?'

'We laugh a lot more. We like being together. Tom was okay at first when he and mum got married. He had his own accounting business, but his partner was a crook, stole all the money, and that caused Tom to give up really, and take it out on us. I can understand why, but I don't excuse his behaviour. Not for one minute.'

'However, when cats suffer extreme stress, as Tom did, it affects the limbic part of the brain. Behaviour then becomes disruptive and unpredictable,' said Grandad, joining the conversation. 'I used to always talk to my clients about what happened to them growing up, or what major changes had occurred in their lives.'

'What do you want to do Stuart, you know, when you leave school?' asked PC.

'I am not sure. I will probably go into business with my mum.'

'What? Be a cleaner?' asked Sly.

'No, although, there is nothing wrong with being a cleaner. No, if Mum needs help from time to time, I have to do my bit. No, it's keeping a handle on all the cleaning materials and servicing the vans regularly. We can't afford to have one of them breaking down. If

I do all those jobs, we save a lot, and that way we increase our profits. We have a loyal team, and we want to pay them well. Mum can pay herself a decent wage now, and we will use the profits for reinvestment as well.'

'You are very entrepreneurial,' said Grandad. 'Good.'

'My dad was a business cat,' continued Stuart. 'I learnt a lot of things from him. His attitude to work, anyway. I could never work for someone else.'

'None of us could either,' said Scooter.

'You know, all the abuse you suffered could have led you to become sad or mistrustful and develop poor mental health,' said Grandad, almost to himself.

'What?' asked Stuart.

'Any Adverse Cat Experiences you suffer, or ACE, as it is known, growing up, can affect you. But it is not only what happens to you; it is also your reaction to what happens to you. Having positive role models and good friends and resilience works wonders. Talking to those you trust is important.' Grandad was looking directly at Stuart, but he knew his words would reach all the kittens.

'Yes, I saw your family, and knew there was another way of existing. I thought I would have to wait until I was older and bigger, but evicting Tom speeded everything along nicely.'

'Everyone needs to feel safe,' said Milo, soberly.

'The one saving grace of getting older, like me,' said Grandad, 'is that you learn to deal with trauma. You will have gone through problems time and time again, and you know that you can survive, and you develop coping strategies. Good ones, we hope. Your stepdad, Stuart, even at his age, did not talk to anyone and he coped by drinking and being a complete nuisance. I hope he has learned to be a better tom now. But none of us is perfect.'

'And that's okay,' said Scooter, 'not being perfect.'

'I think we are perfect, just the way we are,' said PC.

'Our imperfections make us perfect,' said Sly sagely.

'You lot are getting very sentimental now,' said Teabag. She was getting back to her old self and was looking pretty and cute. She was wearing a dress that Teddy had helped her to make, and she looked, well, perfect.

'This is yours,' said PC, handing Milo his headband. 'This helped us to find you. The local dogs took one sniff, and it led them straight to you.'

'Are you saying I should bathe more often?' said Milo, grinning and tying on his headband.

'Very nice,' said Sly, sardonically, not sure a dog should be wearing headbands and shoes.

'No, it suits you,' countered Teddy.

'Food?' offered Sly, putting a large bowl of stew in the centre of the table.

'What I thought we could do this time,' said Scooter, 'is to have a conversation, while we are eating, discussing your homelessness, Milo, and the abuse you suffered, Stuart, and friendships, if you don't mind. I know it's a bit heavy, but I think it would help our subscribers. What do you think?'

There was silence.

'Too soon?' asked Scooter.

'I'm okay with it,' said Stuart.

'Me too,' said Milo.

'Remember, if you don't want to continue, we can stop. Just put up your paw, and we will stop. And I can edit out bits too.'

'We trust you,' said Teddy.

'I think the viewers would want to know what happened to Stuart and Milo anyway. I also told them about all the new skills I was going to learn. Look at this dress, for a start,' said Teabag, holding the hem of the dress and curtseying.

'Let's rehearse a bit first,' said Scooter. 'Tell us about how it felt to be homeless, Milo?'

Sly put some drinks in front of everyone. 'We need to practise eating while talking. Dive in.'

Scooter repeated his question when everyone had a plate of stew in front of them and some milk.

'Well,' began Milo. 'I felt ashamed. I couldn't tell anybody. I had a mix of emotions. Why me? I got angry too. I was determined to find my family and get clues about Battersea, but the longer it went on, I became resigned to being on my own. In a way, I was proud that I could cope, but I was lonely, and some nights I was scared. I tried not to whimper. Only because I did not want to draw attention to myself, and I wanted to be strong. There are foxes out there, you know, but I got on with them, in the end. They helped me get food, and I washed in the pond, sometimes. Not often, I admit. How did you know that I was hiding in the nature reserve?'

'Lucky guess,' said Scooter. 'I knew you loved it there, and it's a good place to hide.'

'I was going to go to Battersea, but I am glad you came with me. I would not have thought to look around, and then we wouldn't have met Greyhound. Greyhound and I hang out a lot now. He volunteers at the Home. He was a sprinter once and won loads of medals. He is quite well off but likes to give back, as he puts it.' Milo makes invisible quote marks in the air when he said, 'give back'.

'Good for him,' said Teddy.

'It is surprising how resilient we become when needed,' said Grandad.

'What about you, Stuart?' asked Scooter. 'It took some guts writing into Teabag's Advice Corner.'

'Kind of,' said Stuart thoughtfully. 'I was going to make something up, but I thought that my problem was a good one, if you see what I mean. I didn't think for one minute you would use it. I am glad you did, though.'

'How did you feel?' asked Teabag.

'To tell you the truth, embarrassed,' said Stuart. 'I was thinking, if my mum heard this, she would be annoyed with me. But she did hear you read out my letter, Teabag, and she blamed herself. She thought she was not a good mother. She is a great mother, but she was so upset that it happened and wanted to put things right immediately. We are closer now than ever. And we are so grateful to you for helping us.'

'And you, Teabag?' asked Scooter, nodding towards her with his chin. Teabag had just stuffed a big piece of meat into her mouth, and could hardly speak.

'As you can see,' she said, laughing, 'I have my appetite back. I look and feel better than ever. I have new social skills; I can dance, cook, and reinvent my old clothes.' She stood up to show off her dress again. All the kittens clapped and told her how beautiful she looked. 'I can't paint, though, that needs a special type of talent. But I do try. I want to thank Teddy and PC for helping me. Oh, and I made this meal today, with Sly's help. What do you think?'

Everyone agreed that it was tasty.

Sly winked at her. 'I am a great teacher, what can I say.'

Teabag licked his head lovingly, and Sly to his embarrassment purred.

'You are a big softy, Sly,' acknowledged Scooter. 'You speak your mind, and never take any nonsense, but you feed us. You take after Mummy Cat, more than you realise.'

Sly was pleased with that and purred some more.

I think your drawings are very insightful, actually,' said Shaky. 'You have the style of an abstract artist.'

'That's not by design, but genuine mistakes,' laughed Teabag.

'She laughs,' observed Sly. 'That is something we hadn't heard or seen for a while.'

'And cut,' said Scooter. 'I recorded it. Sorry. I didn't want you to become self-conscious again. Having fun and doing crazy things is good for us,' observed Scooter.

'Doing crazy things,' thought Milo. 'I wonder?'

CHAPTER TWENTY

Raining Cats and Dogs

The sun shone brightly in the morning sky above a fan of trees, and to the left was a cloud, as vast and black as a mountain range. The magpies were already up. They were pleased to see Milo again and that his leg was better.

Maggie Magpie flew down to greet him.

'I just came to say thank you for saving me the other day when I fell. I brought you some seeds.'

'Oh, no need. I am going to make another worm pie for my tea.'

'The present is not for what you did,' said Milo. 'It's for what I would like you to do.'

'Oh,' said Maggie Magpie, puzzled.

'Could you give me another ride? And my friends too?'

'It would be my pleasure,' said Maggie Magpie. 'Go and get your mates and I will round up mine.'

Milo told Maggie Magpie where he wanted to go and raced around to Scooter's house to tell him the news. He hoped that he would want to come on this trip. It would be so much fun, and a crazy thing to do too.

'Are we really going to see where the Yeading Brook goes?' said Scooter, excited. Teddy wasn't so sure she wanted to fly. 'What if we fall?'

'Don't think about that,' said Teabag reassuringly, but not wildly convinced herself. Teabag thought that this was an excellent opportunity to do something else that she had never done before, and yes, it was mad. 'We will end up on all fours, anyway. We are cats.'

'Not from that height,' said Sly.

'Are we doing this, or not?' asked Scooter, impatiently. 'Because we have to get ready now.'

PC, Teddy, Shaky, Sly and Teabag grew silent for a moment and then each in turn nodded excitedly.

'Hurrah,' said Milo. 'You will love it. You will be able to see for miles and miles.'

'Where are you kitty cats off to?' asked Grandad, hearing the buzz of excitement.

'Maggie Magpie is taking us on a flying trip. We are going to see where the Yeading Brook goes,' Scooter told him, bouncing up and down.

'Can we come too?' asked Grandad.

Mummy Cat looked at Grandad. 'Are you insane? What do you mean "we"?'

'Come on, Missy,' urged Grandad. 'Don't you want to see where the Yeading Brook goes?'

Before Mummy Cat could back out, Milo told her that she and everyone else needed to wear a collar and a jacket because it would be cooler in the clouds, and jeans with belt loops.

When all the cats and Milo got back to the park, they were surprised to see flocks of magpies and blackbirds waiting for them.

'Ah,' said Maggie Magpie. 'There's nine of you. We are going to need more help.'

With a shrill whistle, Maggie Magpie summoned some more magpies. And then, high up in the treetops, appeared the green parakeets.

'Hi Buz, Hi Lu' said Milo. 'JimJam!' They were Milo's old school friends. 'Nice to see you again. Are you taking us as well?'

'Wouldn't miss it,' said JimJam, in a squawky voice.

'We will see where the Yeading Brook goes, won't we?' said Scooter to Maggie Magpie.

'Of course,' said Maggie Magpie. 'And beyond.'

Maggie Magpie flapped her wings for attention and went over to the birds to discuss the best way to go. Finally, they were ready.

Maggie Magpie would be leading. They all had to follow her.

Maggie Magpie told the cats, kittens and Milo that the Yeading Brook did indeed disappear under roads and bridges, but they would be able to see it join the River Crane and see the River Crane join the River Thames. It was going to be a long trip. They would take them all as far as the River Thames and back again. 'The River Crane is wider than the Yeading Brook. Nicer, too, in my opinion. There is a nature reserve there as well. Once we get to the River Thames, you will see murky waters. It is very fast-moving and wide. Along that river are loads of funny shaped buildings. There's a big round thing that goes around slowly. There are bridges and boats on the river, and a big old building with a clock; you'll see.'

Maggie Magpie divided the flocks among the kittens, cats, and Milo. The birds gently held each of them by their collar and the loops in their jeans with their beaks.

'Two more over here,' shouted Maggie Magpie. 'That's right; balance up here. One more for Teddy. Good. Ready? Let's go.'

Teddy shut her eyes and meowed loudly, as she rose into the air. She was sure all her siblings were meowing, too, with a mixture of fear and excitement. Teddy opened her eyes once she got used to it. 'Wow! 'she gasped. 'This is crazy.'

oOo

Scooter at last found out where the Yeading Brook went.

oOo

If anyone happened to look up into the sky, they would have seen what appeared to be large black clouds, high above them. With legs.

oOo

And the evening news reported that it had seemed to be raining cats and dogs over London that morning.

Printed in Great Britain
by Amazon

30411520R00111